I looked, she looked, I looked. Like a piece of lint swooped up in breeze, wafted off towards the horizon, I looked down, the reeling starting. Needed something, some little anything to pull myself back towards the world with, spied one of those little helicopter seeds all weatherbeaten and gray lying on the ground. I snatched it up, staring at it intently, the tiny ragged tears coming and going, clear, and foggy again thru the thickening. I started shredding it, millimeter by millimeter, hey *this* one ain't gonna fly off no more! And suddenly her hand was on my hand and my insides jerked and I looked up.

She was looking — really looking! even further in than before — right at me. And it was like I was a kite torn away that she was re-mooring — her eyes were the place to land. It was like she reached across the light years of outer space and found me in a place where no one's ever seen to in me, and without saying a word, waved me back to the world.

I couldn't believe it. I turned half towards her, not believing it, but it was happening, her face so calm, her eyes on mine. I looked back, looked back, looked back.

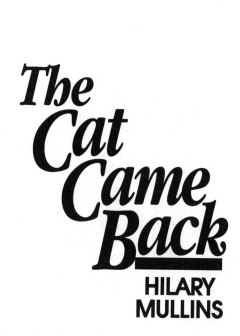

The Cat Came Back

HILARY MULLINS

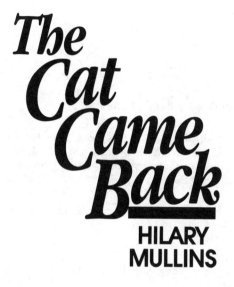

The Cat Came Back

HILARY MULLINS

The Naiad Press, Inc.
1993

Printed in the United States of America on acid-free paper
First Edition

Edited by Katherine V. Forrest
Cover design by Pat Tong and Bonnie Liss
  (Phoenix Graphics)
Typeset by Sandi Stancil

Library of Congress Cataloging-in-Publication Data

Mullins, Hilary, 1962–
  The cat came back / by Hilary Mullins
     p.   cm.
  ISBN 1-56280-040-X
  1. Lesbians—Fiction.   I. Title.
PS3563.U39855C37   1993
813'.54—dc20   93-4757
                                                       CIP

for my mother
and
for the women of Burlington
who saw me through it

About the Author

Hilary Mullins has worked at a number of different jobs, from teen counselor to produce stocker to administrative assistant. Her writing has appeared in various anthologies and journals. A transplant from Vermont, she currently lives in Oakland, California with her lover and their three cats.

January 12th, 1980 *Saturday*

So, what are you supposed to do with a journal? Spill your guts daily? Or start at the beginning? I've tried keeping these fool things before, you know. They don't work. I bet ten years from now, I'm going to come across this pretty little red hand-bound book of a Christmas gift from Mom, and open it up, and this one day, January 12th, is all that will be in the whole thing. That's how all my old journals look — ten or twenty pages scribbled up, the rest blank. Starting with my first journal when I was seven, the year we moved up here to Vermont. Of course, what did I have to write about then? How nice Uncle Philip got kicked out of college for dope dealing and how he came up to live here with us for a while?

Puke. That's the problem. You're supposed to write about how things are really happening. But we're NOT writing about that, about him. Write about something else.

1

I'm so glad I get to go back to school early tomorrow for hockey practice. The thing is I always get so down hanging out here on the mountain. Sure, Vermont is so much prettier than back at school in Connecticut, but there's nothing going here. And Christmas was no salvation, Oma and Opa bringing — yak — Philip up like that. Jesus. He even tried giving me this big "friendly" kiss. Gross! I'm seventeen now, not seven! Doesn't he know I'm too old for that shit?!!

But we're NOT writing about that, remember?

God. No wonder I waited for so long to write in here. Why don't you just come out and say it? I was too depressed! Dad was here for a week and a half, and he kept telling me I should read ahead for the next semester. He didn't get off my back until he left for New York.

I swear my parents are the weirdest parents in the history of the planet. They don't even live together. Well, but that's because if they did, they'd have to admit they have absolutely nothing in common. Mom just hides out here on the mountain, working on her ceramics — I never see her, not ever, I swear, and Dad plays the big corporate lawyer in New York. Then there's me, little Stevie, tall and skinny with a long, long braid, and I hide out too. I want to be a writer, but I don't do anything about it. I don't do anything period. 'Cept get depressed — fuzzy headed. Have scores of nightmares about Kit being lost. The only other thing I do is miss Rik. Damn. I don't know why he never writes me. I understand he has to be careful, but just one letter couldn't hurt! It's not like Mom would notice, even if he is a teacher. Shit. The only letter I got all break

2

was from that new girl, Andrea Snyder, the one who came out for hockey, even tho she's a postgrad who's never played before. Scrappy tho. She might surprise everybody. Her letter certainly surprised me. That she would write me at all. But she's cool I think. What the hell.

January 13th, 1980 *Sunday*

It's so empty in this dorm tonight! I'm the only one on my floor, because Varsity teams come back early for practice. Lonely! I have tried calling Rik ten times since I got back from the rink, but there's no answer. Guess I'll write in here to myself instead.

At least practice was fun. I went over early, and that new girl, Andrea, the one who wrote me, was already there. Just her. She was suited up and everything, and was tightening her skates. She looked happy to see me, and I guess I felt the same way. I sat down next to her, 'cause I thought I should try to be friendly, and I was thanking her for the letter. We started in with the old how-was-your-break-discussion and there I was, talking on, trying to make it sound like I'd had a fine old time, when all of a sudden this weird thing happened. I don't know how to describe it exactly — just that it was as if I suddenly woke up and saw that I was practically sitting on her. Maybe I wasn't really, but it felt that way! I was so close that I could see the fine hairs on her upper lip. In detail. I-yi!! It was time to jump up and grab gear from my cubby the other side of the room.

3

Andrea, meanwhile, didn't seem to notice any of this; she started talking about how she'd gone to this feminist conference that her mother helped put together at Smith, I guess her mother teaches there. Myself, I can't begin to imagine what being at a feminist workshop would be like, but Andrea liked it, that's for sure. She was going on and on about it, and then she all of a sudden clapped her helmet on and got up. Said she'd see me out on the ice.

Hmmmm. . . . the funny thing was that I was both sorry and relieved to be left alone to get the rest of my gear on. Well, but she is a funny girl, I think. So I guess that makes a kind of sense that I would feel that way.

January 14th, 1980 *Monday*

I got hold of Rik this morning. At last. But I had to get over to practice pretty quick so we couldn't talk long. He said he has some work to do this afternoon and a faculty meeting tonight, but that I could come over tomorrow. We have two practices, but we have about four hours in between them. When I told him that, he laughed and said that was plenty of time. It was good to hear him laugh. Hearing his voice made me realize how much I've missed him. I was hoping I'd at least see him at dinner, but when I asked him about it, he said he couldn't make it up to campus before the meeting. Damn. So I still haven't seen him and I've been back a full day and everything. Sometimes this stuff is so frustrating.

Haw! But at least I can write about it in here. That's how I'll finally fill a journal — with complaining!

I still had a good time at dinner tho. A bunch of us from the team sat together, telling jokes, being hockey girls. And the funniest of all was Andrea: her jokes were entire stories she told, everybody hanging off her sleeve and howling as she spun them. I haven't laughed that hard in a long while.

There was such good team spirit at that table tonight. I know part of it is that we get to concentrate on just hockey and each other for these couple of days. But still, if I were any good at this captain bit I'd know how to keep it going. I should call Lisa. She was five times a better captain than me, and maybe she could give me some tips.

I certainly won't go to Granite, even if she is the coach. Most of the girls don't like her, which I can understand, because she seems so flinty and hard. But I think she does have a good heart under it all. Maybe she's gruff, but she does put out. Like the way she gave me extra time and attention when I was first learning to skate.

Put out, put out. Maybe that's what I need to learn to do. Hey, but at least I'm putting out something here in this book. And this is just for me. Complaints and all.

January 15th, 1980 *Tuesday*

So — you were glad to see him, weren't you? Yes, yes, of course! I always am, don't you know.

5

Hmmmmmmm tho

do I write this other part too? It's the jerk in me, I don't really want to say, this other thing, I don't know. Maybe 'cause I'm getting my period soon and that can make me weird. But then again sometimes I'm just weird. Hard to describe, but I know what I mean. It's like I'm wrapped up in fuzz. That doesn't say it exactly, but it's something.

I hope he doesn't notice. Maybe it's not only for hockey I should learn to put out.

January 16th, 1980 *Wednesday*

Sometimes I really hate this place. Like right now when I hear all those fool fake huge and happy hellos going on in the hall. People are still getting back, and with the way these girls carry on, you'd think they'd all known each other since they were little droolers in diapers and were only reuniting now after great and terrible circumstances had separated them for at least a year or maybe ten. It's nauseating. I can't believe they really care that much about one another; it sure doesn't seem like it usually. Such rich girls.

I remember what a hard time I had when I first landed here in the middle of all these wealthy kids. Just a little third former, a fourteen year old kid from the sticks. I really did get some shit too. Like the time someone told me this fourth form girl had said, "Who does that little hick from Vermont think she is anyway?"

God, I felt so alone here then.

'Course later came Granite and hockey, and for a while that felt like salvation. But as it turned out it was joining The Rag that about saved my life. Cuz that's how I got tight with Rik. I didn't even mind that much when The Rag folded fifth form year. Because I was still with him, and that was the most important thing.

Still is. But now, too, because I am a Senior, I try not to look so needy anymore. I know he has a lot in his life, what with being a teacher and a long distance dad and he has all those articles and stories he likes to write.

Wonder if I'll ever dare to really write about him. Maybe once I'm out of this place. Tho I bet he'd rather I never ever committed any of it to paper.

January 17th, 1980 *Thursday*

English looks like it's going to be good this term. It's funny, but at the beginning of the year I thought this new teacher Miss Mic was really an odd bird. I was kinda bummed when I found out I got put in her section. I thought it would have been better to get Phillips, 'cause after all he's an old hand. But there are definitely good points to Mic's being a new hand. Like she isn't reading and teaching Wuthering Heights for the tenth time. She's always letting us know that she's learning along with us. Which I like.

But she's not raw either — the more I study with her, the more I see she's seriously into her stuff, and that she's thorough too. She never apologizes for

7

it one bit. She loves Whitman for instance, and it shows, just from the little she's said about him so far, and by the quick sharpened look she gets on her face when she mentions his name.

Yeah — I'm really beginning to think that the Mic is all right. We were beginning to catch some serious fire in her class towards the end of last semester, and that was great — it showed that what we were reading and talking and writing about mattered. I think most everybody in the class feels this way too, but somehow we're too embarrassed to show it to one another.

Another thing that's great in this class is that Andrea Snyder got switched into our section. That's so she can take an Intensive in ceramics this semester. I wish she'd been with us all along; today in class she made a hilarious joke that had everybody in snorting fits of laughter. Something about Shakespeare and door to door sales, on account of his coming from Stratford-on-Avon; it was the part about Avon see. That girl certainly has a flair with her tongue.

I think I'm not the only one who's glad she got switched into our section. I think John Quinn is too. He was sitting way to my right, but I could see the way he kept sneaking glances over at her. I don't know tho — I can't see Andrea going for a guy like John. He's too straight, a part of that Niblet crowd, too cleancut for someone the likes of Andrea. Actually, now that I think about it, it's hard for me to imagine her with any guy. That's odd now, isn't it?

But then again, you never know, she might say she thinks the same thing about me. Hell, everybody in school knows I've never gone out with any boys here! Little do they know! I hope. I intend on keeping it that way. I'm paranoid myself, I have to admit. I would write more about it now in here if I weren't so friggin nervous. It's like this whole part of my life I can't barely mention anywhere. Heavy duty secrets are a pain in the ass. It's so bad I hardly dare mention it to myself.

January 18th, 1980 *Friday*

God! Granite lost it today! She made Duncan do 4 suicide sprints. SHIT! That is hard core.

But if I had just told Duncan to stop her sulking and slamming her stick every time she missed a shot, it never would have happened. I know what kind of shit sets Granite off, and it's my job as captain to say something. Cuz I knew Dunc was bumming, and I also could tell Granite's fuse was getting shorter by the second.

Of course I certainly understand why Duncan would be bummed — in the new lines Granite posted today she bumped Duncan from first line to second; put Andrea on my left wing where Duncan used to be. Which is a drag for Duncan, sure, but she didn't have to be such a baby about it! And besides, if she'd work harder, the way Andrea does, she wouldn't be getting bumped in the first place.

I still wish Granite hadn't been quite so hard on her tho, the way she was yelling at her to skate harder the whole time, never let up on her at all, even towards the end of the third sprint, when you could see Dunc was getting exhausted. But jesus, Granite's the coach, and I'm not going to tell her how to do her job.

But that Andrea wants to! Is she crazy or what? Somewhere during D's third sprint, she sidled up to me, nudged my shoulder, and asked, "Can't you tell Granite that you think that's enough already?"

I couldn't even think of how to answer her. Finally I just shrugged and said I didn't think it would help, that the next thing I'd be out there too. Andrea came right back saying something like if that was what it took, then maybe we should all be out there. I must have looked at her funny with that, because she shrugged and turned away. Well, what was I supposed to say? Does she really mean that? There's no way.

January 19th, 1980 *Saturday*

Well, at least our Saturday schedules coincide nicely, me with the first three periods and him with the first two. And today practice was in the late afternoon because the boys had a game, so right after third period I met him out back behind the dorm and off we went. This is the longest chunk of time we've had since I've gotten back. He didn't waste a minute but got right down to it, and afterwards I stood around in that high ceiling-ed kitchen, leaning against the counter, while he made grilled cheese sandwiches and tomato soup. I was telling him a little about Duncan and Granite yesterday and also about what Andrea said to me.

Lord knows I needed some feedback about the whole mess, and he gave me some good perspectives I think. 'Course he's not always nice about the way he puts things, but his points are good anyway. He's never been crazy about Granite, that's for sure; he's always saying she's in a constant state of premenstrual tension. I wouldn't put it that way myself, but I guess he can if he wants to.

Anyway, he pointed out that usually confrontation is not the best way to deal with someone as volatile as Granite. 'Specially when that person is in a position of power over you, like a boss or coach. It's the whole hierarchy that's against you he said and "power politics" is what it's called. That means it's Granite who has the power, not me. So I should think whatever I want but at the same time make sure I cover my tracks and therefore my ass. Don't say anything, don't tangle with her head on.

The more I think about what he said, the more I see that that's how he's survived so many years at this school. I mean, he doesn't really believe all the garbage the way some teachers do. I think he gets by pretty well doing it too. And actually that's how we pull off this thing we do — we just keep it to ourselves. That's the key. Don't go making any jokes to let off steam or anything, like the way Andrea seems to when she doesn't like something.

As for her, Rik said she looks like one of those rebels who's always looking for a cause and will make one up if she has to. She's the next James Dean, even noisier, he said. I said she's a girl, how can she be? But he just laughed.

So maybe a girl can be a James Dean type if she wants, who knows? I've always been kind of a tomboy myself. But I do think Rik is on to something more there. It does look to me sometimes like Andrea Snyder is looking for a fight around this place. I hear it in a lot of those jokes — the way they run just this side of outrage. She does stay enough to this side tho so that everybody still laughs. But I don't know. I mean, she is incredibly funny, but it makes you wonder what she might do some day. And her tracks wouldn't be covered at all.

Not me tho, not me. It's not worth it. Not at all. Rik's right.

January 20th, 1980 *Sunday*

Super Bowl Day. I really wanted to watch with my friend and eat grilled cheese sandwiches again — cheese, cheese, more than a food, it's a state of mind, it's a metaphor, OK? I don't know how else to say it! "I got cheesed," oh, snort.

But anyway, no, he had to work on an article today. He always seems to be working on something when I call. Of course that stuff means a lot to him, I know. So I ended up watching the game in the common room on the top floor. A bunch of the team was there too, Diamond, Duncan, Jessie, Pat, and Andrea Snyder. Jessie had had the foresight to order out for a couple of pizzas, which was good, but I don't know, I was out of sorts. Everyone else seemed quite jolly tho, all sprawled out on the rug in one another's arms, having a gay old time I must say, so chummy it was a regular slumber party. Which made me feel even greyer. You'd think the captain of of the team would know how to jump in, but me, I'm such a strange stiff stick. By the end of the game, I didn't even care that the Rams got thrashed. It didn't seem to matter.

Duncan and Snyder, by the way, had themselves in a particularly happy pile at the far end of the couch. I wonder how it is Snyder can get all buddy-buddy with Duncan like that. You'd think Duncan would resent Andrea for being on first line now. But I could see nothing even vaguely resembling resentment there. In fact they were having themselves nothing short of a perfectly swell time, cuddling up close and laughing a lot. Liddy wasn't anywhere around, but I bet she won't like it when she sees Andrea horning in on her best bud like that.

But — maybe Duncan goes for those James Dean types. Who knows? Who cares? Why am I even taking the time to write about it?

January 26th, 1980 *Saturday*

What a scare show these last few days have been! The game today too. I am such a bad captain. We were in tatters out there on the ice, and I had no clue about what to do to make things different. Dudley skated right over us. Girls were out of position, giving lousy passes, barely daring to put any shots on goal. Including me. Somehow we couldn't click as a team. What a disaster! We must have looked like a bunch of startled St. Bernard pups snuffling around with our heads down, wondering where in the world that puck went to. Pathetic.

Granite was good and steamed too. She gave us a lecture in the locker room that could not be beat. She would have had all of us out on the ice doing ten Suicide sprints if we hadn't been in the middle of a game. She wasn't very nice afterwards either; she snapped something about how we were a disgrace to the Bristol school, and stalked out of the locker room, slamming the door hard as she went. Some of the girls started shaking their heads, and some wouldn't hardly look up. Duncan spat out, "What a bitch!"

I had no idea what to say, so I didn't say anything. I'm such a lousy captain. I think the only thing left tonight is to go to bed. It's too late to be writing about such depressing stuff.

January 27th, 1980 *Sunday*

This afternoon as I was sitting on my bed drinking a Coke and eating a Danish I pirated from the dining hall, there came a sharp rap rap at my door. Surprise, surprise! In walked Duncan and Liddy. Can you believe this shit! They came marching right in, planted themselves in the middle of the place, down on my gritty rug. Said they needed to talk. I sat down too, feeling the color rushing up into my face, wishing I could crawl under the bed. But there was no way out. They started in, taking turns, talking in these insistent voices, asking me what I was going to do about "the crisis."

Stupid me, I asked, "What crisis?" I could see their respective impatience with me, skinny Liddy cross-legged with that tightness in her mouth, a thousand thousand words I knew I didn't want to hear festering behind those pursed lips, the stockier Duncan pulled further back, leaning against the dresser, shaking her head the slightest bit.

Liddy put a hand on Duncan's hand, took over the speaker's role. Liddy's big on being the speaker. She announced to me that in light of Granite's recent "abusive behavior," some of the girls were seriously considering leaving the team. Some of the other girls being Diamond and Patty and Karla and — of course — Andrea Snyder.

Liddy was going on and on about how bad Granite is, and I, meanwhile, wasn't saying a word, no agreeing nods or anything even. I was backing up bit by bit on my butt towards the bed. Suddenly Duncan burst out, "Oh, c'mon Stevie! You don't think Granite is an asshole for what she did to me?!"

I got up on the bed. I said something like if Duncan had only paid attention to what kind of shit sets Granite off, she could have avoided the whole mess. I thought I was being reasonable! But Duncan got really pissed anyway. She asked, her voice raising and sort of shaking, if I like the way Granite screams at us, if I really think it's OK for her to treat us the way she does.

God I hate it when someone gets all bent out of shape like that. I stumbled into something about how it must be difficult for Granite too, and how she has this big pressure on her to make us a winning team. Duncan all the while was shaking her head, like she thought I must be the biggest simpleton alive, and I hated her for a hard fast moment. Then Liddy was rubbing Duncan's head, telling her to give it a break.

Duncan was still bent, I could tell, but she did stop, and Liddy started in again, doing her best to smooth things out. She's smart. I could see how she was working to bring me around to her point of view, not horse me off. Duncan on the other hand would hardly look at me. Liddy said all this stuff, but in the end it boiled down to the fact that they thought I, as captain, should go and talk with Granite, explain how these team members feel they should be treated better.

I couldn't say no. I really couldn't. Duncan and Liddy were right on me. And I am captain, and being a go-between for the team with the coach is one of the things I am supposed to do. So what could I say? It wasn't like I had any bright alternatives. Liddy made it clear thru everything she said that if something doesn't give here, this group of girls is going to quit. It doesn't even matter if I agree with them or not, the threat remains the same: we'll lose a quarter of the team. Christ, I don't know why they have to make such a big deal out of this.

How am I ever going to say that shit to Granite?

Like who is the worst to face up to? Granite or the other girls?

God I hate this. I don't even want to think about it anymore.

January 29th, 1980 *Tuesday*

Rik was Mr. Come-Thru-in-the-Lurch today. I called him, kind of upset about this hockey stuff and he came right up to school and picked me up. He said he knew what I needed and he gave it to me too.

Maybe he was right. He came and got me, didn't he? But I don't know! I'm such a fuzz head. Let's just say it was OK, all right?

So, anyway, afterwards I still wanted to talk, and he indulged me. What he had to say wasn't that different from what he said the other day, all that stuff he calls "power politics." He said the last thing I should do is confront Granite directly. He said I should talk to her privately, flatter her first and then let her know that some of the girls on the team are having a hard time and that I'm not sure they'll last the season at the current pace, couldn't she let up a little, o pretty please.

All the while keep stroking, he said. Appeal to her vanity. Remember that old quotation (this he said laughing), 'You can flatter people so much that they won't believe you, but you can't flatter them so much they won't be pleased.' The cheese man said the most important thing I can do is please her.

Well, I don't know if anybody could ever please Ellen Grant, but I am going to try. Tomorrow. Good luck to me!

January 30th, 1980 *Wednesday*

God! We don't call that woman Granite for nothing, I'll tell you that! She is some stony and hard. I felt so small in there with her this morning that it was like I wasn't really even there. So much for the stroke routine. I did manage to say something about how I was worried that not all of the team was going to hold up, how maybe we should let up on them some. I said some bullshit thing too about how that seemed like the thing to do even tho I certainly valued the stuff she's taught me about sportsmanship and playing your heart out. All that sort of thing. No response back from the hooded eyes, and I kind of trailed off, feeling foolish.

She picked up a sheaf of papers, gave them a sharp rap on the table top, straightening them. "Is that all?" she asked. I shifted in my chair, said that I guessed it was. "Good." She almost barked it out. "But thanks for keeping me abreast with developments. I'll see you out on the ice." She bent over the papers, and that was that, four seconds later, there I was, back out in the hall, wondering what had happened.

Jesus, why can't I even talk!! If Liddy and Duncan ever knew! Or Andrea! Who, wouldn't you know it, came up to me at lunch to ask how it went. I told her I didn't really know, which is not a lie exactly, but when she said she was sure I had done my best, I felt like the crummiest liar in the whole world.

But it turned out OK anyway — no credit to me, I'm sure. At the end of practice — which was a little tense, but not bad — Granite announced a short meeting after showers in the locker room. Yikes! I thought for sure she would come in and lower the boom on us. But the boom never hit. Not really. She came in with the same stoniness I saw this morning tho, so it wasn't like she was honey lips. She drew herself up in front of us and said she wanted to reiterate to all of us that being on the Bristol girls' hockey team means coming out on the ice every practice ready to work hard. She said she understands the pressure we're all under with our schoolwork, but that when we get out on the ice, we're here to skate and to play hockey to the best of our abilities. Period. And that was that. She didn't even wait to see if anybody had anything to say. Poof! She was gone.

So — I think it could have been worse. Not everybody thought about it that way, of course. But Andrea was grinning! She said, "Man that woman sure could use some therapy!" ?! Before she was all worked up, and now she laughs it off? I don't get that girl.

January 31st, 1980 *Thursday*

God. I wish I could be more like Andrea. She goes whooping up and down that ice, throwing herself into the skating. It's not just with skating either. It's with everything she does. I don't think she ever has to think about putting out, she's already there in the thing. Well, when she's not being testy, that is; I've seen her get that way. But it makes sense; it's like she's making sure first, and then, when she is, VROOM! off she goes.

I guess I think she's pretty cool. Even tho she was a little weird towards me the next day or so after that thing with Duncan and Granite. But now she's being friendly again. I like that, I might as well admit it. I really should get it together to take that walk downtown with her. If she still wants to, of course. The thing is, the couple of afternoons she did suggest were ones that I was already supposed to be with Rik. I didn't tell her that, of course, I made up stupid lies that I felt guilty about. Christ! Sometimes it seems like my whole life is one giant lousy lie.

February 1st, 1980 *Friday*

I got my paper back from Mic today. It wasn't so hot; she gave me a B. OW! She wrote that I need to work my points harder, take them to some resolve. I think I know what she means, but I don't know if I can do it. Seems like ever since this last holiday, I don't read so clear, don't write so clear, can't come up with one single miserable line of poetry. Sure, I've gotten depressed over break before, but this time I'm still not back to normal. Usually it does take a while, but this is getting out of hand! I am so out of it!

It happens with Rik too, I know it does. How do I say this? The way that even when I am there it's like I'm not really there. Isn't that weird? But I

20

don't know any other way to describe it. It's that fuzz stuff; that's all I can say. And I try so hard not to let it show. I don't want to hurt his feelings, don't want him to think the wrong thing. Thank god I can hide it good.

God, sometimes it seems like I'm spending my *whole* life hiding *everything*. Well, at least I don't have to do that in here.

February 2nd, 1980 *Saturday*

What happened??????!!!!! You want to know what happened? I'll tell you what the hell happened! Today everybody on the team played shitty. We lost the game, and the coach's ex-favorite player lost her head all together, played like a fool.

What more do you need to know!?

Jesus, jesus, I hardly feel like talking to myself. But spew it out, puke it up in this book and maybe you can leave it behind on these pages.

OH OW OW OW OW OW!

All right, OK,

there we were, scrapping around the ice, lost, and Rider Academy was walloping the puck up and down in circles around us, scoring. Granite was yelling, just the way my father does when you can't be sure that he won't lose it all together and start flailing on you. I had already been out on the ice forever and a half and was very tired; had just missed a pass, was chasing the puck, scooped it off the boards, whirling, and was skating up what seemed like a miracle mile of clear ice, when suddenly Diamond and Liddy are in front of me, waving madly, and I'm thinking how strange it is that our defense are playing this far up, when the framework cracks, and shatters, and I get that I am skating the wrong way about to shoot on our own goal!

Fuck! I spin around, the puck goes slithering off my stick, and I'm gaping, until two seconds later, a ref whistles an off-sides call. Meanwhile, I'm still spinning, my head woozy — like that one time I got wasted on hash and couldn't fasten to anything. Then I looked up and saw the big north window and the rink clicked into place around it. That was a relief! But I could hear Granite screaming at me to get the hell off the ice.

I came slumping over the boards, tried jumping over, but Granite was pumping her arm, motioning me her way. Her face was the color of a lobster in a pot. I came up to the door, and she started in, blistering me, shouting stuff about how could I be so stupid, such an idiot, what a moron. I was bobbing my head, mute, and next she —

I got to write this too

— she grabbed me by the shoulders and was shaking me. Hard. Like a sack of potatoes, bits of her spit flying into my face. The words coming out with those bits, like, what the hell was I thinking? Didn't I know how to skate?!

It was so weird. I was entirely seized. I don't know if I could have said a word to save my life. I just stood there, staring at the crowsfeet around her eyes — which I've never noticed before, all these crinkly minute lines, and meanwhile blast after blast exploding in my face. It was so strange — I have to

22

describe it better; it was bizarre, because I was there getting shook like a rag doll, but in another way I wasn't there at all, and that was because far back in my head, some part of me had disconnected like a phone line yanked out of the wall. It was like I had floated off and was watching her from three thousand miles away, how her mouth twisted, opening and shutting.

Then out on the ice the ref dropped the puck and Granite released me with a little shove. I reeled off as far as my legs would take me down the bench, plomped down, left my helmet on, and proceeded to watch the rest of the game from right there on the bench, looking neither right or left, just hanging in there with that three thousand mile away feeling going like a buzz in my body. I could feel the looks flying around me, but I sure didn't look back at anybody. And in the locker room they left me alone too.

Good thing. It's much better to stay three thousand miles away sometimes.

February 3rd, 1980 *Sunday*

Andrea was just here. I can't say I was particularly sociable, but enough already. I don't know what she wants from me, but I want her to leave me alone, alone, alone.
ANDREA SNYDER LEAVE ME LEAVE ME BE!!!!!!

But wait, but ho! I'm getting ahead of my little story-self here. Shouldn't we start with the morning? How I skipped brunch, had a Coke for breakfast.

23

Then read some history, albeit in a spotty fashion. What was it about it now? Two brothers in Russia . . . oh well, it will probably come back to me tomorrow in class, soon enough. Went out back to wait for Rik, he was late, tho once we got to his house, he suddenly got into rush rush mode.

Jesus. I know I shouldn't say this. I know I shouldn't. But I think we're too far gone here, I think we are.

I just wish that cheese were the cure — all that Rik always seems to think it is, because if it were, I've had enough to be born again, I'm a pepper crammed to bursting with creamy stuff. But I don't know — somehow I can't seem to feel it! Lord knows I could use the resurrection. If only my body wouldn't betray me, I could drink up at that fountain of rejuvenation. I must be broken; I don't work, not ever, I'm stuck, locked and bound behind this huge wall. Nothing moves, we're all dead back here, stench of rotting flesh stewing in itself, can't get clear. I wish someone could get to me, split me open like a ripe pod of peas, so I could tumble out in the warmth of their hands. Can't somebody break me? I can't do it myself. If I could, I'd take my guts and crack them open on a rock, watch them pour out over the ground, gashed sac of stomach juices and mire of blood.

Good god, we are getting carried away tonight, little Ms. Stevie, what a spectacle you make of yourself!

Enough already. Stop.

What I was going to say is that we were lying there after, and he wanted to sleep I think, but I kept coming out with bits of the story; I just had to talk about it. So he ended up indulging me, and once I had gotten it out, fragment by fragment, he stroked my head and said, "Lie low, baby, lie low." While I was thinking about it, he fell asleep.

I couldn't sleep at all tho, and by mid-afternoon the sky clouded over, we both had work to do, and he drove me back up to school.

And here's where the real fun began: I was greeted, on my return, by a short but carefully-worded note from Liddy announcing that she and Duncan and Andrea sincerely appreciated my recent efforts to work things out with Granite, but they didn't, given her "outburst" yesterday, think that there was any reason to believe she would ever change, and hence, therefore, they were leaving the team.

"We are not quitting, just leaving a bad situation which we do not think will improve."

Yeah, right. Well. Later, it's just before eleven, I'm standing at my dresser, bathrobe on, fumbling for the soap, and there's a rapping at the door. It's Andrea Snyder. Who, in one way, I was surprised to see, but in another way not. She's the kind of person, I think, where a note would not be enough. But the note was enough for me — more than enough! I didn't want to talk to her after that note. I know what I think, and she's not going to sweet talk me out of it.

But didn't she give it the old college try! She asked me how I was doing, and I said OK. A little, loaded pause, and she asked me if I'd gotten the note, and I said yeah, and then she wanted to know what I thought about it. All this time she's just at the threshold of my room, and I'm backing further away, towards the window.

Perhaps I was sullen. For one thing, I didn't like her catching me in the bathrobe. It's this filmy red thing Dad got me at Rube's downtown in New York, sort of a cross between a kimono and a smoking jacket. I always feel like it doesn't draw properly together above my chest, and it's so slippy against my skin, it feels like it could slide off my body anytime. That Andrea, she's looking hard at me, and I'm clutching that bit of red satiny stuff to my body. God.

Andrea said she hoped I hadn't taken the note the wrong way. She said she really enjoys skating with me, but that she thinks that Granite has a serious problem.

"Yeah, but she didn't touch you, it was me she grabbed!" Outburst! Jesus, why didn't I keep my fool mouth shut! But that girl, she gets to me, I don't know where my head goes when I'm around her.

Right back she came, saying, "Well, maybe this time, but I don't feel like waiting around to see if I'm the next one!"

So all right, I used to think I knew how to stay out of Granite's harm's way, but really there's no way to guarantee it. Saturday proved that. You can't skate and not make a few mistakes anyway, and with Granite, mistakes you pay for. That's just the way it is. But maybe I can make fewer mistakes if I try harder. If only I could learn how to put out more. That's my problem.

I wanted to try and explain some of this to Andrea, but I didn't know how. And she was going on anyway, getting so emphatic. She knows what she believes, that's for sure! Never a moment of doubt for Andrea Snyder! She was saying, "You know Granite doesn't give a damn when she gets flailing like that. She'll use anything to take all that piss and rage out on. I'm not sticking around for it!"

It was right at this point — I don't know why exactly, that I lost my head all together, started babbling–shouting at her, half–crying, half–yelling, telling her that that was easy for her to say, she hadn't been on the team for three years, she's not captain, that I couldn't just up and quit. And did I leave it at that? Of course not! I told her how her leaving was going to make things that much harder, who was going to tell the jokes now, keep things light? Who was going to skate my left wing?

And what did she say back to me after that stunning outcry? "I don't think of it as quitting, thank you!" I saw in the way her lips jumped a little that she was feeling defensive. But at the same time she was wrinkling her eyebrows, slanting them sideways down in a way that screamed out "PITY!! PITY POOR STEVIE!" It looked to me like she thought she shouldn't let herself be angry at such a pathetic creature, and for a flashing second I hated her, stood there, furious with the feeling. I couldn't believe I had actually told her all that! What a stupid thing to spill those beans, to let her know that I would miss her! It's not like me to burst out with stuff like that. Then I didn't hate her, I just felt entirely foolish, stood there in my red robe, stricken. I couldn't see where to go at all.

So I snatched my towel off the hook and started for the door. Andrea about fell over turning around, backing out, saying "I don't want any hard feelings between us if I can help it!" I was in a rush, I can tell you, because the tears were burning up in my eyes, and I didn't want her to see those, no way.

I choked out, "Maybe you won't be able to help it!" And then I was in the shower, twisting the handle, shaking my head furiously beneath the hot water jetting down.

I know she's lying about that liking to skate with me stuff. I know she is. What kind of a fool does she take me for anyway? Pitying someone is not the same thing as liking them. Not at all. I don't need her fucking pity.

God, why do I let her get to me so much anyway?!

February 4th, 1980 *Monday*

Something's going on here. I couldn't get myself over to practice this afternoon. All morning it was sort of that three thousand mile away feeling. After classes, I went back to my room and flopped on the bed. Doze, doze, doze, and I noticed that it was getting on quarter to three, time to be moving, but I could not will myself to it. Then — when it was *really* time, I watched myself start to pretend that I wasn't doing what I in fact was doing. Fell back off to doze-land, and when I woke up it was past five, and in my head, I could see the rink, empty.

Meanwhile, in my room, it was dark, not quite dinnertime, and I started in on tonight's English:

Moby Dick. Which I've been reading for hours now, getting ahead of the homework, always a good thing to do. But there wasn't anything I wanted to do anyway; who am I trying to kid. It was hardly a matter of virtue.

I haven't eaten, don't feel hungry, it's more like if I tried eating, I'd feel sick. It's too late to eat now anyway. Nothing left to do but go to bed.

But I still have one more thing to write. It's really weird tho, so I'm kind of scared to write it. But I've got to try putting it down here anyway 'cause Mic is always saying the best writers make a vocation of getting at the real. And I'm beginning to think that *that* is why I'm writing like a maniac in here most every day. It's more than complaining! So — here it goes: I feel like some part of me has fallen down deep onto a hard floor inside.

There. That's it. And down deep on that hard floor there's this thing this place this feeling that don't want to budge.

But that's crazy, that's really crazy. It's maybe OK to write it, but tomorrow I *got* to get to practice. I can't afford too much of my strangeness out in the world, I don't think.

*February 6th, 1980 *Wednesday**

I quit hockey today.
That's all there is to say.
Don't ask me for a word more.

29

February 7th, 1980 *Thursday*

Today the Bristol girl's hockey team played Rose Hall, losing badly to them, and I wasn't there. I was in the Headmaster's wood paneled office. Bellows was leaning his long large body forward over his desk towards me, talking with the utmost gravity, wanting to impress on me "the grave and serious consequences" of my "actions." He wanted me to explain my "hasty and impetuous decision." But I could barely rouse myself out of my stupor to talk to him at all. Really, I couldn't even begin to explain it to him.

God, I wish I could.

But at least I can try and make some sense of it in here. Even if it is only to myself — telling myself what's real. So. I woke up Tuesday morning and the worst of that fuzzy weight was on me, bad as it has ever been, makes it hard to walk, to talk, eat, be alive. It was no trick to get a blue slip out of the nurse, and I stumbled back to my room; covers up, and I was gone, the hours blurring by, and some knock-kneed fourth form girl I've seen cowering around the halls in barrettes brought me my dinner, representing that little do-good group that's authorized to bring food out of the dining hall to sickies like me. She tried her sweet nervous best to ask me how I was, but I was stone, it's no good trying to talk to me when I'm like this, it's beyond me. I tried reading for a while, but that was beyond me too. I turned out the light, rolled over and listened to the dark all around me, coming down heavy on me,

the same heaviness I woke with again the next

30

morning. When I finally got him over the phone, Rik couldn't — or wouldn't — see me, and I dragged my ass around to classes, in this strange turning walking panic, but acting like everything was fine fine fine.

That's what I do. And I went to practice. Actually got myself over there, suited and everything, trying not to stare at the empty cubby Andrea left. It bugged me. It bugged me that it bugged me. I didn't want it to. But I was so heavy it was only one more thing. Dragged out onto the ice, in a sort of stupefied disbelief that I was managing it, and felt this moment of — well, thrill almost, that at least I know how to fake it so well. That I could make myself do it. That I wouldn't have to spend the rest of my life in bed after all, washed up, washed down to the bottom of the ocean. I mean, what if I die there? Die here?

Keep talking. Make noise.

So — we went skating around, warming up in our turns around the rink, and that heaviness was a permeation thru my whole body, every inch a ton bearing down. We started into our usual routine of drills, and I was waiting on line for this one passing drill, and Granite was doing that hollering that she does, she says, to re-create the "stress" of a game. I was next up, standing, shifting my weight back and forth, from one skate to the other, listening, maybe for the first time really hearing that flinty broken-bottle sharp edge in her words, the way she hurtles them like broken glass at us. Really hearing it, that smashing.

Something in me
snapped.

31

I don't know. I found myself turning around and skating off the ice! It surprised me, and it certainly surprised Granite. She stopped mid-barrage and stared at me like the roof of the rink had just fallen in and was crumpled in pieces between us.

I didn't know what I was doing exactly, but I was leaving, that was for sure. Granite snapped out, "Where do you think you're going, Roughgarden?"

Without thinking I said this silly little thing my mother always says: "Away." Granite skated for me, was on me in a few hard strides, clamping a hand on my arm. Christ! I didn't once know this whole time what I was going to do before I did it. I hissed, "I'm quitting this miserable team so get your goddamn hands off me!" She recoiled, like I'd spit in her face, this shocked surprise blasting her features open. I felt her vice grip fingers loosen on me, and I twisted out of her grip and skated right off that ice, and that was that. No more No more No more!

I'M FREE!

February 8th, 1980 *Friday*

Father called this morning. Evidently Bellows phoned him, and so he knew about the whole thing. He was, he said, "very concerned." My gut caught sharp and hard. He went on about how he didn't think I understood the gravity of my decision, about how I was letting my school and my coach and my whole team down. He said I was letting *myself* down. I wasn't saying anything much. He didn't seem to notice, went on and on. Started into one of his favorite lectures with me, the one where he tells me that I go out of my way to be a non-conformist. Then he said how happy he'd been that I seemed to have "outgrown" that and was finally "testing my mettle" in a leadership position. But now my sheer bull headedness was making me throw it all away.

I don't know why he is always talking to me about me developing leadership qualities. I sure as hell haven't been skating all these years because I wanted to be captain of the team. I've been skating because it's fun. I love turning on one edge to a screaming snowy stop, I love the speed, I love playing with the other girls, joking around and sitting on the bench spitting.

There's another reason why I loved hockey too. For a while anyway.

But I couldn't tell him about that. Hell I couldn't even tell him the stuff that should be easy to say. I stood there, mute as a silo.

He went on and on. I finally had to say *something*! "Yeah, but I was co-editor of The Rag before it folded!" That's all that came out. Way to go Stevie.

He sort of snorted and said he meant serious school activities, that The Rag had obviously been just another way I'd "flaunted" my non-conformity.

I think that pissed me off a little bit. I didn't say anything tho.

But anyway after about twenty minutes of this kind of talk, my old man was getting himself pretty worked up. Damn worked up. I could hear it in his voice, he was approaching that edge of his. The only thing that saved me from getting all the way blasted was that he had to make a conference call. Phew.

He couldn't ring off without a parting shot tho, doesn't it figure. He said something about how he hoped I would be "mature" enough to reconsider my decision.

I didn't answer him.

February 10th, 1980 *Sunday*

Andrea came and sat with me at brunch this morning. God! My heart in my mouth! Right up there with my waffles, and as squishy too. Why do I get so nervous around her? Damn! I felt so undone! Even tho it was obvious to me that she was bending over backwards to make up, I still felt strung like high-tension wires inside.

That's the hard part. The good part is that I think she gets why I quit. I think it maybe has a little to do with the stuff she said to me that night, working its way into me gradually. But I didn't tell her that. And she didn't ask me how it was I turned totally around from what I told her that night; she kept it light. She was just trying to be nice and make me laugh, and it seems like she can always do that.

I, meantime, managed to half-apologize, stumbling and saying it sideways, for the way I bit her head off the other night on my way to the shower. She said it was OK, that she had understood I was in a bind. She's funny! 'Cause next she laughed and said that if I signed up for intramural hockey and played with her and Duncan and Liddy, they would give me plenty of opportunities to work my "pent-up hostilities" out on the ice.

What kind of hostilities does Andrea think I'm penting up anyway?

February 11th, 1980 *Monday*

So there I was right at the outdoor rink at three, and next thing I knew, Andrea was clapping me on the shoulder, plopping down on the bench next to me to pull on her skates. One thing I have to say: she sure is cute.

Liddy and Duncan were psyched too. It was fun out there this afternoon. FUN. Imagine that. Williams is pretty wacky on the ice, but then again, he's pretty wacky in History too. This afternoon he got us all going with his antics, and sometimes just to be crazy he would break out of the ref role to play and once he even picked up the puck and skated into our goal with it. The guys who play are pretty cool too, not too macho or anything. Those are the kind of boys I can deal with.

And I like, I really like playing with Andrea again. She is fun. Really fun.

Some little thing sticking with me — Rik said, hey great if you're not off every afternoon and night at practices and games. The slivering flashing that stabbed thru me for an instant. I know I'm usually the one who's after him for more time, how I'm looking to talk a lot, but — well, I don't want to have to give over all this new time either. I mean too much of even a good thing is still too much, right?

Right?

February 12th, 1980 *Tuesday*

Ellen Grant in the hall today. Upstairs. I saw her from maybe twenty feet off, coming towards me. My head started crashing and my heart started banging and I looked for an open classroom door to dive for, but the two at hand were closed with classes going on behind them. No outs.

There was this one long lanky fifth form boy loping along maybe ten feet ahead of me, but when he passed Granite, it was just her and me with this charged space that shrank, concentrating its charge as it did. AGGGGH! I drifted further towards the opposite wall, developed an intense fascination with the squaring pattern of the floor at my feet. But DAMN ME! I *had* to look up into her face as we passed. She was half-looking my way, but it was like I wasn't even there, I was nothing there at all, NOTHING NOTHING NOTHING! Her eyes were as blank as a freshly-washed blackboard.

Ran down the stairs and all the way back to the dorm. I felt like I could have cried and screamed and smashed things. But I didn't. I lay on my bed face down for a while. But I was kind of a jerk in hockey today. Pushed a few of the boys a little harder than I should have. Well, but it is the way they play with each other. Still, if a girl pushes them like that, they won't do anything back. But

36

hey — if I'm gonna be a bad girl I might as well make the most of it.

February 13th, 1980 *Wednesday*

ALL ABOUT GRANITE AND ME
BECAUSE I AM NOT NOTHING THERE

She's the one who found me. I was fourteen. It was winter term, third form year, and I was at the rink, by myself, skating for the hell of it. I was a pond skater back then, but not falling over or anything. She came in, and I saw her notice me. She called me over. Asked me why I hadn't come out for hockey. When I couldn't come up with an answer, chipping at the ice with the front of my blade, she asked me to come out.

I remember I stood looking up into those pale pale eyes — she really has the most amazing eyes, you can get lost in them for days — and I was just sort of nodding to whatever she said. Who cared about Intra-Hoop? Not me! If she was the coach, I'd play. I was at practice the very next day. I wasn't very good at first, but I was more than ready to work at it. Which is what I did. Worked and worked. And Granite coached me, even gave me extra time after practice. I loved it, the attention.

Then in mid February, when I guess she decided I would stick, she said we had to get me some good skates. So we took one early Thursday afternoon, drove to Hartford to the sports shops and I bought a new pair of Super Tacs with the money my father had sent me. I remember I carried the bills stuck in my shoe. After we got the skates, Granite took me for a milk shake at this old soda counter she knew from her college days. I remember that afternoon so well — there was a thaw, and it felt like spring somehow, run-off everywhere down those grey city streets. She was extra nice to me and I was so happy — being with her, walking next to her, this confident proud woman. I remember I lived off that afternoon for days.

My god, what a schoolgirl I was! But still! I worked so hard for her! And even after Rik came along, and I made the switch over (like you're supposed to) I still worked for her! I always did. That's why I don't get it, her treating me like that when I've busted my butt for her all these years. It wasn't even my idea to be captain; it was hers. I did it for her. 'Cause even tho I was older and had been with Rik for quite some time, there was still some of that old feeling kicking around. There always is, I guess.

yikes

Jesus Stevie, why don't you just admit it to yourself, say it already, it's not like anybody is listening here! All right, all right, so I was sort of in love with her back then. It's true, I really was. We're talking love-love. Oh god.

Shit, that's enough for tonight.

February 14th, 1980 *Thursday*

St. Valentine's Day. I just got back, a full minute

before curfew, and I wouldn't say he's sentimental or anything, but he did sort of get into the spirit of the occasion. Not mushy but saying, "oh, what a fitting way to celebrate. ah. oh." Stuff like that.

Myself, I wish I could have been a little more into it. I have had Granite on the brain all day. I kept bringing her up without meaning to. He finally got annoyed with me, said I was wasting my time thinking about that "frustrated castrating bitch." Man, he really puts things a certain way sometimes. He wanted to know why I couldn't just enjoy this, and this, and this, and then he was off with it and there was no more room for words.

Yeah, well, Happy Valentine's Day to me. Writing that stuff yesterday — maybe I shouldn't have. It's brought it all back to me — the way I used to feel I mean. But I'm seventeen now, not fourteen! That stuff doesn't fit anymore!

If I could just learn to relax more when I'm with him. But damn, I can't figure out if I should be relaxing more — or maybe figuring out some way to put out more.

Fuck Granite anyway. Rik likes me. He likes having me around. I'm not nobody with him.

February 15th, 1980 *Friday*

Out during IntraPuck today I was in that really weird sullen mood I get into sometimes. I know they all think I'm a pain in the ass.

That Andrea Snyder tho — she's a glutton for punishment. She was after me again for that pizza outing. I can't imagine what she wants with me, but she came up as we were getting off the ice, said, "Hey."

I said, "Hey," back and she started right in asking about pizza and saying how we could go skating on the lake before too. I was feeling too weird to stand there and talk with her, so I said yeah, OK, tomorrow afternoon, but right now I really got to get on that English reading. And made good my escape. That's all I want to do these days. Escape. Everything.

But hey, maybe some distraction will do me good. Every day I check the board to see when girls' hockey practices, and when that time rolls around it about drives me crazy. What if that afternoon I had jumped over the boards, and not given her the chance to get her hands on me? I *know* what she's like. I know how frustrated she feels sometimes. I could have spared us both the scene maybe . . .

I couldn't go back now tho. Not after I left like that. There's no room left for pretending nothing happened.

February 16th, 1980 *Saturday*

Rik wanted the afternoon, but I couldn't back out on Andrea again. It was at lunch. He was kind of grumbly. I felt bad, didn't see any way to please them both. God I hate it when that kind of thing happens.

So. But. I had fun anyway. Andrea and I met

down at the waterfront with our skates, sat on the logs together pulling them on. That Andrea is nice. She is really nice to me. I can't figure out what I've done to deserve this.

Or what she wants —?

But anyway — skating on the lake — well I liked it very much. I wasn't really expecting to have fun, 'cause I've been feeling so weird lately, but there was something about all that space stretching out around me, lake, lake, lake, and sky, sky sky — endlessly it seemed. I had to go fast, in long strides, swooping. Then circle back around to Andrea who was loping along. Her cheeks were red under her red cap. She didn't care that I went fast. She was having fun too. At least it looked that way to me.

Then — finally — we went for that pizza. The restaurant was warm and filled with that steamy pizza smell. We both had that big hunger and munched. But we talked some too. Andrea is into asking questions. She asked me the question I thought she would: the sowhydyouquit question.

I stumbled, starting, but then I told her how I made myself go to practice what turned out to be that last time, how something in me snapped hearing Granite yell, how that part in me just marched the rest right off the ice.

Andrea was nodding, looking over the brim of her waxed cup of soda. Wry, almost pained smile.

"Well, I'm starting to think that that same part of me knows I don't have to take her shit," I said.

"Well, I think you're right," she said, "you don't have to take her shit." And then her smile opened like a light moving up her face.

Damn, she sure does act like she likes me! 'Course I don't know that for sure, but it looks that way. What would it be like to have a friend my own age around this place? I don't even know.

February 17th, 1980 *Sunday*

I had this great dream last nite. I've been feeling it all day:

Me and Andrea are in my room. We have all these crepe paper streamers in our hands, and we're dancing. Dancing with the streamers, prancing around up on the bed, the streamers bright flowing bands of color thru the air, and we're filling the room with that motion and with our dancing. Dancing together. Breezy, like we're flying too. And I think to myself, "Wow! This is like never being alone again."

God, what would it be like to feel that in real life?

February 18th, 1980 *Monday*

Things with Rik tonite were weird. Oh god. Maybe I'll try to write about it tomorrow.

February 21st, 1980 *Thursday*

Cold, cold cold! I hate these cold snaps. It's like I can never get warm enough. Except in the shower or in bed. Which makes getting up in the morning all the harder. Yak.

Have hardly seen Rik at all this week — Katie's up. He brought her to dinner last night. She is such a cute kid, sandy-haired and freckled, half scruffy, half dolled up with her calico skirts. So in earnest too; she really keeps him on his toes. Better than I ever have, and she's only seven. But me, I'm such a fuzz-head anyway, what can I expect.

*February 22nd, 1980 *Friday**

coldcoldcoldcoldcoldcoldcoldcoldcoldcold
coldcoldcoldcoldcoldcoldcoldcoldcoldcold

freeze

harden

crystalize

turningfinallytostone

icerockhardnobudgenobouncenobend

dead

February 23rd, 1980 *Saturday*

So — once upon a time there was a huge beast that lived at the bottom of a vast lake. She had lived there a very long time. It was quiet under the water, and calm and blue green. With her bottle-neck eyes the beast could still sometimes see what was going on above the water line, back on shore. It was a manageable life, spring, summer, fall.

Winters tho, were harder. Often the lake froze solid, from one side to the other, and from end to end. Then, thru all that ice, the world looked very fuzzy and far away indeed. In the winter the beast sank to the very bottom of her inland sea, scraping herself along the deepest ledges.

Come spring, things would begin to loosen, cracks begin to show. In the spring, the beast was known, in her hunger for a change in altitude, to come all the way to surface, poking her large nose and thick eyes out, bobbing slightly with the waves. A few times, spotting her from shore, a few other beings, perhaps guessing at her loneliness, had paddled out in boats to talk with her.

The beast, however, was very shy. She would listen, gratefully, to their stories, sometimes even asking for songs. But then, as if from some unknown signal, she would suddenly blink and submerge. And perhaps not be seen until the next spring.

But oh! oh, the winters! The winters were long!

February 25th, 1980 *Monday*

Well, it's like Andrea wants to be my friend. I mean, I think she does. Maybe she just has this policy about being nice to charity cases tho. I mean, really, is there anything about me that Andrea could honestly like?

Well, everybody knows that I'm supposed to be smart. But I'm not very good looking or anything. I guess I'm all right, but nothing much. And maybe I am smart, but it's like I can't do anything with it. My brain sits there like a dead fish at the top of my head. I'm not that kind of sharp in action that Andrea is. Or funny. And nowhere as good looking. I mean, once in a great while Rik compliments me when I dress up, but it's the clothes that make that, and it's never clothes I really like anyway. So where does that get me? Andrea, on the other hand, looks great, no matter what she's in. Just something in the way she moves, all that goes on in her face. I don't know.

So look, she's all that. And then there's me. Can she really mean it? Really? But maybe I should check it out? I mean, why not? Am I afraid that a little kindness will kill me?

Poem for class —

Lake Skating

Charcoal smudge figures
receding in a dream of distance,
the ice fishermen's shanties crouch
within shouting space of shore,
vague whispers eddying at my back
as I skate, blades jangling across
   the thaw-scarred surface.
All around the earth holds
the lake in its lap, encircling
with bare-treed mountains.
But the grey of the late winter afternoon
seems to rise from the ice, and over —
spreading, tinges hillsides.

I have long been beyond hailing
shanties or shore, the distance
drawing me on; I forget the promised
time of return with the watch in my pocket.
Two miles out the creaks and booms
begin their song, but any danger
is only imagined: "jest the lake stretchin'"
the fishermen always say. I drop
to my knees and lie flat out
on my stomach, dreaming of the dragon
they say lives in the lake. Its huge cries
explode above, charging the air
with an embracing sorrow. I look up

to see ice and sky merging in endless grey;
on all sides empty space expands.

Cold ice gnawing at my cheek, I imagine
this numbness taking hold, hardening
to an impossibility of return —
Strange — how now the sure scent
of the fishermen's wood fires
finds me out, a tiny twinge
of warmth nudging in my nostrils.
Slowly I get up, skate, gathering
speed towards shore; wave
to a fisherman standing by his shanty.
He waves back with one hand, holding
in the other an iridescent and thrashing fish.

February 27th, 1980 *Wednesday*

I dreamt that dream about Kit last night. Just like I did during break — dreamt that I'm looking out the kitchen window at home, and I see her prints in the snow, the way she went. I follow her tracks with my eyes a ways, but then there's a big drift, crested along the top, covering them all up. I know she's lost, and I'm too late to find her. It's all my fault.

Rik wanted me to come over this afternoon, but I had already promised Andrea way back on Monday to play hoop with her this afternoon. I think he was a little put out. It's a hard thing, pleasing people.

Andrea doesn't seem that hard to please tho. We met up around three and slogged thru the snow over to the old gym. That locker room over there sure feels ancient. Smells that way too. A few lockers here and there hanging open, socks over the green slitted metal doors, girls' bras hanging on the hooks outside.

We had a good time playing hoop. I did anyway. Andrea seemed to be enjoying herself too. She laughs a lot. Her eyes light up when she quips at me and I joke back. Sometimes she'll throw her head back and laugh out loud. Hard. Today she looked like a girl having a good time, that much I can say. 'Course she knows how to have fun whatever she's doing, I think. We didn't play seriously; we just played, bounced the ball and ourselves around, not bothering with a score. That's how we do it in IntraPuck too, none of this deadly grave stuff like Granite.

After an hour or so we hightailed it back to the

dusky locker room and showered. I wanted to keep joking around and splash her, but I didn't dare. On the way back to main campus we climbed up that one low sloping roof on the backside of the gym and jumped into this big snowdrift a couple of times. Fun! Really fun.

I guess that's the thing I want to say about hanging out with Andrea: it's really FUN.

February 28th, 1980 *Thursday*

Rik sat with me at lunch today. That's sort of unusual for him. He said, "Where you been?" I didn't know what to say. 'Course it's not that I haven't been to meals, it's that I haven't been making my usual every other evening calls, checking in, seeing when we can get together. So now here he was, asking me that question, giving me that sly smile of his, head cocked to one side. Do I like that smile? I don't know. Somehow it's as if it wants to pull something out of me, nudges at me sideways.

Well, anyway, I told him that — besides Wednesday of course — I've been spending a lot of time this week on my Baudelaire paper for French, doing critical research and biographical reading on Monsieur Poet Francaise in the library. A lot, I said. He made some comment about what a little scholar I'm getting to be, but he left it at that. I felt bad. Because even tho the first part is true, the second part isn't. I have been doing some work on that paper, but also I've been hanging out in the Senior Cup and Butts room most every night after dinner.

Drinking tea with Andrea and Liddy and Duncan. I've hardly ever done that, hung out with people in my class. I have always scurried off to Rik's before long, one way or the other. This is different now tho. I want to see who the hell these kids are already. Before we graduate.

...But maybe that's not the whole thing? Because it was like I couldn't tell him that was how I felt. I don't know why really. Maybe I'm trying to get back at him for not spending enough time with me while Katie was here? And I just can't admit it to myself? Much less him. I don't know: it was like I couldn't talk to him straight on at all. Something kept bumping up in me — bumping up between me where I was sitting on one side of the table, and him, perched across on the other. He kept smiling that smile, nudging me on, without coming out and saying IT. He likes being subtle he says. There wasn't anybody else at the table, till Jeanie came along after a while, but he always likes to play it safe anyway. He said, "Sunday would be a good day for a cheese fest, don't you think?" I said yeah, and that's when Jeanie came, so we didn't talk about it anymore. I don't know, I felt weird about it. I don't know. I don't know.

Maybe I'm weird and that's all there is to say about it. But still — I do know that I want to hang out with my friends, not always have to be slipping off to meet him so we can do our after dinner thing. Or our afternoon thing, or the Sunday morning thing either. It's important to me to spend time with him — don't get me wrong — but there is other stuff I want to do now too. Hell, it's practically Senior Spring, even if it was only 23 degrees today. I want to get warmed up for the season we've all been waiting for!

February 29th, 1980 *Friday*

NEWS FLASH!!!!

Mic *loved* the poem. She really did! She said it was "poignant" and "wonderfully full of beautiful images." She said she especially liked the ending, the iridescence of the fish in particular. The best tho was that she said I have the writer's gift: "the ability to create a piece that has two levels that work together simultaneously — the surface, apparent level, and the deeper level of metaphorical meaning." Huh. Not bad for a dead fish brain I guess. Mic also said that she hopes I take her mini-course the second half of spring term when the English classes all break up and do those special courses. Mic's is going to be creative writing. Of course. I think it would be great to do it. I thought so before, but now I think maybe I'm good enough, which is the difference. It might be really great. Really great.

Today is Leap Year Day. Mic said in class that on Leap Year Day women can ask anybody they want out on a date. A "date"! What a strange concept, going out on a date. What are you supposed to do? I don't know, it's not my forte, that's for sure. But if somebody pressed me on it, I mean, hell, it's a once in a four year opportunity, if I had to do it —— Oh god I'm getting silly here! But I know who I'd ask to hang out with me!

And it's not Rik either!

Ooops!

OK, OK cut that out now! Get serious here! All right. Dad called today. I guess he finally got it that I'm off in a week for break. It's the first time he's called since I left the hockey team. He's like that when he gets bent out of shape — he won't call for a while. But he wants me to come to New York anyway, like I usually do, for the first week. I said sure. Probably the less time in Georgeville the better. Plus I can work at the office and make some money too.

The phone conversation was a tad weird tho, I think. I guess he's still irked at me for quitting. The only thing he said about it tho was this sharp little thing about how he hoped I was using my newly freed time to study. I ignored him, went on to the next thing, but it kind of bugged me. I get good enough grades, why isn't that enough?

But anyway, in a week, I'll have money and time coming.

But what about fun?

March 2nd, 1980 *Sunday*

I had a really fun day with Andrea today. Really fun! But right now, I'm feeling this static in my head. Attack of The Killer Fuzz! The thing is I had kind of told Rik I would do his "cheese fest" with him today. But rather than calling him first thing, I stayed in bed a long time, just kind of dozing, and then went right to brunch. It was getting late, and I was very hungry, and then, once I was there, Andrea came to sit with me, and she looked great in her jeans and in that wool sweater which is about a hundred colors all swirling around together. Well, I was just happy to see her. And while we were eating, she said, "Hey, what about another action-packed adventure today?" I had my glass of orange juice to my mouth, and this stabbing flash of my promise to Rik went thru me, and I kind of choked. I don't think Andrea noticed, but who knows? I could be kidding myself on that one.

I put my glass down and said, "Sure! What do you want to do?"

"Let's go play pinball!" she said.

"Pinball?" I said. She was nodding away. Pinball has never been one of my things, but I didn't tell her that. I said sure instead, because I thought what the hell, I wanted to hang out with her and what we did wouldn't really matter. It's just fun to be with her. I like it, that's all.

We both had a few things to do first. So I said I'd meet her in her room in forty-five minutes. I went back to the dorm and showered, and then took as much time figuring out what to wear as I did showering. Sometimes it's hard to get it right — not that we're even dealing with fancy clothes here. But anyway — I wore my best old jeans with all the patches, and that maroon sweater I've had since I was fourteen with the sort of turtle neck. Plus my hiking boots and my thick red hunting jacket. I didn't want to look too dolled up or anything, but I hope I didn't look too much like a hick either. Maybe it's sort of silly to think so much about what you're wearing. I usually don't care that much. But today I felt like an action-packed adventure called for some careful clothes selection. That's all.

So I was re-braiding my braid, using the mirror, and seeing my face there in the glass, I knew I didn't even want to call Rik. I was thinking, "What am I doing? I told him I'd call." But the thing was — I don't know what the thing was actually. I just didn't feel like calling. I sort of just put the whole thing out of my mind, how could I do that?! And now here it is, ten-thirty at night, and I still haven't called him. I know he won't call me — he doesn't think it's cool to call me at the dorm. What am I going to tell him when I see him? I've never done this before. I better think of something.

But I don't want to worry about that now. I want to write about my day with Andrea.

We started out walking slow. It's two miles into town, and sometimes we talked and sometimes we didn't. The day was getting greyer and greyer and by the time we got to that little shop that's half ice cream and soda shop, half pinball and pool place, the sky was spitting this cold wet half snow, half rain stuff. We ducked in, went up to the counter. Andrea got a root beer, I got a milk shake. I like those best, mix chocolate and strawberry in together.

Andrea is so cool. It was so much fun just to watch her, how she played pinball, hauling on the steel knob, and leaning way, way over, talking and yelling and laughing. And how she played pool too, the way she bent over the table top, sighting along the flat green towards the cluster of shiny balls, the way she slid her stick back and forth twenty times over her thumb before she actually shot.

We played and talked. Outside the rain had

started pelting down in earnest, and we decided to play the best of three games of pool. Nobody else hardly came in, we had the place to ourselves, which was great. Andrea was asking me questions about growing up in Vermont, and I told her stuff, just skipping over that one part about P. I never tell anybody about.

That Andrea Snyder knows how to ask you questions! She knows how to take the answer to the last question you gave her and see where else it might go. She's a real good listener too. It was almost scary, don't ask me why!

So I asked her some questions too, like what it was like growing up in Boston and what's it like now to live in Northampton and have your mom teaching at Smith. I wanted to ask her if she ever sees her dad, but I wasn't sure that I should, so I didn't.

It sounds to me like Andrea likes things all right in her life. She's not real thrilled about going to Smith next year, but she gets such a break on tuition 'cause of her mom teaching there, that she's going to try it. She was really lucky and got this special scholarship to Bristol for a post-graduate year, which she needs she said, because Smith said she had some catching up to do before she enrolled. Not that she isn't smart or anything. She's really smart! But she says the schools she's been to are not so hot. So. And she said she's not terribly thrilled either about being at Bristol, but that the experience is worth it: "seeing how the other half lives," is how she put it. I didn't get what she meant by that, and rather than pretending that I did, I asked her about it. She said, "Oh you know, the rich, the filthy rich."

I said, "oh." Took my shot and missed altogether, handed the cue back to her, and popped out with, "Do you mean like me?"

She said, "No! Not you! You're different! I don't mean you at all!"

Inside I thought, phew! But I didn't say that out loud of course.

Somewhere in all this we lost track of which balls were whose, but we cleared the table for the third time anyway. Neither one of us wanted to go back to school yet, so we ran thru the rain to the pizza parlor and split a small pizza. I love that place, always that warm steaminess inside, the smell of bread baking and the walls come in close and the booths are red and hold you in cozy-like.

We ate, and the pizza was great, and I had this moment where I was chewing and looking across at Andrea — who was chewing one minute and doodling cartoons on her placemat with a purple pen she had in her pocket the next, and I felt so goddamn happy I couldn't quite take it even. She was looking down right then, lucky thing. I don't know how I would have explained the look I know must have been on my face.

We were taking our time, eating slow, sometimes talking, sometimes not, when surprise, surprise, Mic came in with Mr. Jackson, Mr. Theatre par excellence. Hm, I wouldn't think he'd be Mic's type, he's sort of swishy or something. Which I don't mean in a bad way or anything. Just I'd think Mic would be more into outdoors types or something. She never says anything about having a boyfriend tho. Probably because she doesn't think it's anybody's business but her own. Which I guess is right.

Jackson was cooler than I remembered from Drama Class last year, he made a couple of cracks about Bristol while they were waiting for their pizza, talking about the curfew and restrictions — me and Andrea weren't really supposed to be still out in town because it was getting after dark, but Mic and Jackson didn't care at all. Which is really cool. But they did give us a ride back. In the car, Mic was asking us what we'd been up to, and Andrea was telling her, and Mic somehow thought it was very very funny that we had been playing pool. She cracked right up and laughed a good minute anyway. Maybe because it's not the kind of thing kids at Bristol seem to like to do. They're all such snobs. I'm glad Andrea's not like that! And that she feels the same way about me. I think maybe I finally have a friend around here. A friend my age.

But what am I going to tell Rik about today? Damn, I really should have called him this morning. But I really didn't want to.

March 6th, 1980 *Thursday*

Saturday break starts! God it will be good to get my confused little self out of this joint! I need some time to figure out this stuff with Rik. I'm feeling so weird about him these days. But let's not write about it, OK? I'll write about it once I get it all figured out.

March 9th, 1980 *Sunday*

Well, there was that dragon in the god-awful lake, lonely like I said. But she was not always alone there, for her solitude in the lake was sometimes broken by afternoons, sometimes whole days, with an adventurous sea captain who had long ago blundered inland in his battered little boat. He loved to tell tales of high adventure on the vast oceans of the world and the dragon began coming aboard his boat to hear them. She was not such a big dragon, she was rather small in truth, the captain actually having quite a greater girth than she. People think all dragons are large and horrible, but it is not true.

Once she was aboard, the captain began feeding her: thick porridges he would ladle out from a huge iron cauldron and dark bread he cut and buttered with a massive oak handled knife. The little dragon would begin to eat, and he would watch and stroke her scaled sides with the flat of his blade, admiring her long neck out loud and talking of love. Certainly the knife made the little dragon nervous, but she had never heard such praise before.

She began coming back for more, the captain's soup and stories and his flattering words. One late evening he brought her down below deck to show her his cabin and the great furnace glowing red-hot.

Years passed in this manner, afternoons at his

table, hours below in the room next to the ancient groaning furnace, its flames spitting and sighing, the waves scudding overhead. Fall, winter and spring, and on the afternoons she did not go, she cast about thru the uncaring waters, sometimes staring toward the empty shore. Then she would head back for the boat. . . . .

One afternoon, a stranger appeared on the shore, and below her in the water, the dragon could feel her land legs growing, a new fever taking hold in her gut, but how could she say no to the sea captain who had fed her, stroked her, taken her aboard when there was not another soul on the watery horizon?

Come, he commanded, and she did, for how could she not? But the ship tossed and heaved her that day — or was it possible that she no longer knew the way to walk on those decks? And the journey down the creaking wooden steps horrified her in a way she had not felt horror, not in years, and the furnace there swelling beside them, and the captain was a teeming weight bearing down, she could not move, and held her breath, going away somewhere deep into a bubble of air she held clenched tightly in her dragon teeth — until he had rolled away, and she found her feet and headed for decks and the open air, miles and miles of it, a blue sky so vast above she dove off the boat, back into the huge and sleepy arms of the lake, the new one calling to her from shore. . . . . .

March 10th, 1980 *Monday*

Who me, depressed? I think I wrote yesterday more than I thought I knew. I don't know how that can happen, and yet there it is. But it's sort of like I put it down in another language. Probably couldn't write about it any other way, tho the words scald the page as they are! Nothing I want to think about for very long, that's for sure. Writing about it yesterday is enough for the meantime.

Today I worked at the office. It was boring, and hard for me to keep my mind empty enough. I hate spending all day in that closed empty space. Hell, the windows aren't even made so you can open them. Hit the streets at the end of the day and it's a shock to come out into the air.

God, I am so depressed, I'm trying to hide it from myself. Thank god Dad is still laying off of me. 'Course he's just damn happy to see me working all day, head down, yessir, that daughter of his, she ain't no goof-off after all.

i think i miss Andrea.

March 12, 1980 *Wednesday*

This working at the office is getting to me.

I HATE IT

God I *do* miss Andrea.

It was so hard saying goodbye to her at school. I couldn't show it tho. We were standing by the bus, next to this dirty shriveled snow pile, and she was shivering in her red chamois shirt. She looked so beautiful to me, standing there in the sunlight, the way it caught in her hair in glints, brought out that ruddiness in her face. Oh god. But I was in such a fuzz head, that stuff with Rik the night before. Still — I waited until the last minute to get on the bus, and as I was going up the metal steps, this fifth form boy was jostling me from behind so I couldn't turn and wave or anything. Once I got to my seat, I couldn't see her anywhere — she was gone. She probably was glad to light out as fast as she could. Because I was being so weird. I bet she doesn't miss me for the same reason —

I'm too weird to miss.

March 13th, 1980 *Thursday*

HOORAH!

I just got off the phone with Andrea! It was great! She called me here! And now I'm going to her house! God! I can't believe it! When I heard her voice on the other end, I kind of knew it was her, but that seemed so impossible I couldn't believe it. But it was her! I didn't even know what to say at first, but then I asked her how she tracked me down. She said she'd called Georgeville to get my number. We talked about how our vacations were going. I told her how boring the office is, tho I didn't really tell her about how bad I feel there! Don't want her to be thinking I'm some storm cloud of a character! She said she was sort of bored too. Then she told me she'd been wondering if I would want to come for a visit: "so we can be bored together," she said, laughing.

All my insides jumped at once. Boy, I tell you, if I'm not some storm cloud, I'm this bundle of coils waiting to be sprung any minute. Why can't I be calmer? But this time I can't help it. I am so psyched! We can really have fun when I go there. This will be so much better than sitting around alone in Georgeville.

God it was great talking with Andrea on the phone. We've never done that; we've always talked in person. But tonight she was a voice in my ear, a slight huskiness sometimes breaking into a staccato laugh. She's so cool. I can't wait to see her.

March 14th, 1980 *Friday*

It's a good thing I have this trip to look forward to, or I don't know how I would have made it thru the day. As it was, I barely survived, and that was by living off my anticipation. I can't wait, I can't wait. Now I've got two hundred dollars stashed away in the back of this book.

I can't wait to see her!!!! Her face, those eyes, how she laughs, the way she walks, everything about her, I can't wait!!

March 15th, 1980 *Saturday*

Wouldn't you know he couldn't leave it alone, that we couldn't be together a whole week without him laying his heavy daddy trip on me? Wouldn't you know it?

But I don't care, I don't care, I'm outta here tomorrow. Get me away from these lectures about developing leadership qualities and the importance of competition to the formation of my character. Who wants goddamn "character" anyway if it lands you in a stuffy office with a world of people who can't look each other in the eye? It's such a game downtown, and he thinks it's the only world, the real world. I know he thinks Mom is a silly dabbler with her ceramics: there, there dear.

He was sitting there under his great brows, in all force of seriousness holding forth, about how I have so much potential, how I have to make something of myself, how it will be one of the greatest disappointments of his life if by the time he dies I haven't done it.

God!!!!

He went on and on! I just sat there, english muffin getting cold on the table in front of me. On and on about how concerned he is that I quit

64

hockey, how irresponsible it was for me as captain to do that. Ouch! That was the sting that got me! I told him he wasn't there and that he didn't know what it was like. He said he knows what responsibility means, that it means not running out on people. I said I didn't run out, I was chased out, and he said I couldn't blame other people for my mistakes.

But the thing was, it wasn't a mistake! Try explaining that to him tho! Well. I didn't even try. I just let him go on and on until he had said everything he had to say. Maybe I should have tried, but I could feel myself getting all worked up, about to blow, cry, lose my shit, and I had to check it. Just sat there, sat on it. 'Cause you can't get out of control like that. Especially with him it is lethal, I'll tell you. I'm not going to be like Mom; whenever they fight, and she starts getting upset, he tells her she's too emotional. He stands there like a glacier, immovable and icy. And meanwhile she's dissolving into a jelly mass.

That's not me. I'm no mound of jelly losing it.

And someday when I really learn to get a grip on myself, then he's going to hear about it from me. Gonna really hear it all right. 'Cause then I'm going to get all the words right.

March 17th, 1980 *Monday*

I like this apartment, the bare old wooden floors and the big windows that the sun pours thru, colors everywhere on the walls, the dried flowers on the table, all these clippings on the refrigerator, cartoons, stuff from newspapers, postcards. Andrea's downstairs in the shower, her mom's still out. I'm up in Andrea's room, this top third floor space, all angles sloping down. Her bed is a mattress on the floor, something my mom would never agree to! under this one place where the ceiling comes down but then opens out towards a window that looks down onto the street. It's neat, kind of what you would think of as a fort if you were a little kid.

Which I'm not, anymore, but still, there's that sense to it. I like it. I like it here.

Andrea met me at the bus station wearing that wool hat with the reindeer on it. Her cheeks were all red, and I walked down the steps and we both were grinning like mad. That bursting feeling — it was hard to look. Well.

She was driving. She has her own car because she's had after school jobs the last few years. It's this clunky green Ford Pinto, vroom, vroom! We drove around some, and I was feeling pretty shy, I have to say. She might have been feeling the same way, I'm not sure. Then we came here, and she introduced me to her mom, who says I should call her Lois. You can tell these two are mother and daughter — Andrea's this wirier version of her mom. Not exactly of course, but the resemblance is definitely there. Tho Lois was wearing this wraparound skirt when I first got here, and I've never seen Andrea in any kind of skirt at all. Or a dress. She's just not the type I guess. But they're still pretty similar in other ways. They both have those dark curls tho, and the sharp nose. 'Cept

Lois's eyes are brown, brown, brown. As for Andrea's eyes, well we know about Andrea's eyes.

I am so happy to be here! The rest of my vacation isn't going to be like the first of it, nor like my vacations usually are, I can taste it. This is going to be some fun for once. Even if I am still feeling sort of shy. I'll get over it soon enough.

March 18th, 1980 *Tuesday*

Early morning in Andrea's room. God, how funny to wake up next to someone! And it was weird last night too. Like I wanted to share the bed, but didn't want to either. Both at the same time!

What's the big deal anyway?

Last night we were sitting around the kitchen table for the longest time, playing cards and talking. About growing up and everything. Well not everything. There's that old shit about Philip that I never tell anyone, and who would want to hear it anyway, but there are other stories to tell, certainly, so I told them. Andrea had some good stories herself to tell, the way she grew up kind of poor, 'cause her dad kept losing jobs from drinking too much. Then when her mom left him, they were still poor, on account of her being a single mom and going back to school.

I asked Andrea if she misses her dad — she never sees him, hasn't laid eyes on him in years, tho they know he's still living in Boston, and sometimes he sends her a card with five bucks on her birthday.

She said she doesn't really miss him, because mostly he wasn't very nice, but sometimes she misses the good stuff about him, when she was really little and he was fun. The times he'd bring her treats and play with her.

But she said they wouldn't be where they are today without her mom. I guess Lois is a pretty ambitious woman. She's very sharp. She did a whole lot on her own, getting thru school, getting her Phd in Anthropology, and then landing this job at Smith. I asked Andrea if her ambitious mom wants her to be like she is, a professor or something. Andrea said she doesn't think that's so important to her mom.

"But does she want you to be an artist?" That's what I wanted to know. Andrea laughed and said, "My mom doesn't mind me being an artist per se, she just doesn't want me to be a poor artist!" And we both laughed, hard. It was like we both understood something about it, something I can't put my finger on exactly, but something that was enough to really crack me up. That's what being with Andrea is like, something we both understand but that I can't put my finger on exactly. And still, it's enough, all right. Oh very much enough!

March 19th, 1980 *Wednesday*

We went to Emily Dickinson's house today. Her room so still and hollow, but brimming over with her, that poised presence, white intensity. I could have stretched out on her little bed and dreamt of her all day long. Andrea seemed to feel it too.

After, out driving: warm sun of spring, the road rolling under and swelling up to meet us, Mt. Tom and the view, the looks we give each other when we see something and it's like we both know, yes, it's this way, this thing. We talk too tho. We talk and talk and it flows like a river back and forth between us.

She: wiry, sharp, energy, energy, energy. Intense, black curls, the light in her face, teal eyes that watch me, open wide, narrow when she's confused. Strong hands — I just noticed them today. Don't know how I could have missed them before. Maybe it's not the only thing I've missed.

March 20th, 1980 *Thursday*

Morning again. She likes to sleep. I like to watch her. It's the only time I can really do it, hold my eyes to her face; somehow I can't look enough. It's like there's something I'm trying to see, and I don't even know what. After a while of that tho, I had to jump out of bed and grab this book here. I didn't want her to see me propped up on one elbow next to her, looking, looking. I shouldn't be doing it probably. Much less writing about it.

But it is time to write, time to draw myself together in these words. I'm going to call Mom tonight and tell her we're driving up tomorrow, staying till Sunday. Dad wouldn't be too crazy about the idea of us driving ourselves that far alone, but I'll fix that by not telling him. I don't think Mom will mind, she's always said I should have friends up more than I do.

Andrea is the best. The Best. I love being with her. She's the best friend I could ever have. Yeah, this is what they must mean when they say close. Just this way I feel with her. And that maybe she feels with me — ?

Then too, there's this other feeling, it's hard to describe. Because if I can stay with this, trying to write about it, there's this thing in my stomach, a pzazzing that gets fizzing sometimes. When? Oh ————— oh, I know when, *those* times. Times, times, times, when, when, when!

God, I'm going to fizz over just writing about it.

March 21st, 1980 *Friday*

This thing last night, this thing that happened.

Lois took us out for pizza, which was great. She is so smart, and knows so much about ancient history and pre-history and cultures of tribes and stuff like that, all the Margaret Mead kind of stuff. She calls herself a feminist too, so maybe being a feminist is more respectable than I thought.

Anyway, afterward, oh gawd, we went to this ice cream shop, and the ice cream was so good. We were sitting at a booth, licking away, and there were these two women, like college students, over in the far corner. They didn't look that different from Andrea and me: I mean they were in jeans and sweat shirts. Definitely older tho. Not a lot, but still. But anyway, they were having a really good time, laughing a lot, taking licks off each other's cones. I was watching them. I always watch people when I'm out. I like to try and figure out their story.

So yeah, I was watching. Andrea and Lois didn't seem to be. Leastways I don't think they saw what I saw.

Which was: part of the dark haired woman's ice cream fell out of her cone and went splat on the table, and the other one with the really really short hair said, "Aw!" and she was trying to scoop this dark clump of ice cream up with her spoon, but she missed and it went into the dark haired woman's lap instead. That cracked them up. They started laughing, laughing, laughing. I was laughing too, tho to myself, and Andrea and Lois were going on about something. All of a sudden, like out of nowhere, the woman with the short hair leaned over and kissed the other woman!!!!!!! On the lips. Hard. Not any friendly peck or anything, I'll tell you that. It was definitely a lover's kiss! Like the next minute they might start doing it right there or something, it had that kind of charge.

I couldn't believe it. I must have been staring too, because the short haired one looked over and right back at me, the calmest, coolest gaze. I looked away of course, really embarrassed. Then Lois was asking me something and I had to say, "What? What?" 'cause I was so flustered.

But that's not all. As they were going out, Lois waved this big friendly hello to them, and they waved back. She said they were her students! I couldn't believe it! I wonder if she knows about them. I didn't dare say anything. I mean, would she still like them if she *knew*? Maybe she'd want to flunk them or something.

I'm sure glad Andrea didn't see all that. She might think I had the wrong idea in my head if she saw the way I was staring at them. I mean, I really like Andrea lots and lots and want to spend time with her and everything — but that stuff — *that* stuff is really something else. God, it makes me so nervous just writing about it, like the fizzing twenty times worse. Maybe this is enough writing in here for the morning anyway. We should get moving here pretty soon too, get on the road.

God how she sleeps!

March 22nd, 1980 *Saturday*

What is this fuzzy crap stuck in my gut this morning? Strange — like dream hangovers from dreaming about Kit last night. For hours and hours, that same nightmare where she's lost, but this time I go running out into the night to find her. Running, running, running, and just when I think I'm never going to find her, that the night is going to swallow me up too, I hear her. She's caught up a tree, crying, but the tree is in an incredibly dense forest, and I can't figure out which tree she's in, and I keep running around, craning my head up to see her. But I can't, and I'm crying, and she's crying, and I can't help her. I can't help her.

Yak.

Let's try something cheerier, what do you say? How about dinner last night? It was great, because Mom liked Andrea a whole lot. Well, how could you not, but anyway she did. Asked her all these questions about her sculpture, and I heard Andrea say stuff about her art that I've never heard her say. 'Course I'm not an artist like Mom, so she knew to ask questions that I wouldn't think of.

It was fun tho. You'd think I would have woke up in a better mood, because it all went so well. I don't know. Maybe I'm just allergic to this place, the way it gives me Fuzz Attacks.

March 23d, 1980 *Sunday*

Morning coming round too early again. I don't want to be here anymore. I dreamt about Kit again, for hours and hours it felt like. And never any way I would ever find her. I was awake a lot too, lying there trying not to move, my whole body in itchy quirks, listening to Andrea breathing in her sleep next to me. I don't think I woke her up. I felt weird. But it's weird up here on the mountain, it's like the house is empty even when people are here and if I stay, every night will be twisting dreams in dark woods. Kit lost forever.

Maybe this summer I can get Dad to pay for one of those wilderness trips. Or something, anything. I'll rot if I stay here. Or worse.

Yuk. I feel like shit. Yesterday we went cross-country skiing out back, and I was practically hallucinating. I couldn't tell Andrea, I felt so crazy. But it felt like there was somebody behind every tree. Somebody, somebody, who? Some man, I think I know his name.

Jesus! Get me out of these woods!

March 24th, 1980 *Monday*

It was weird, strangely hollow somehow, to wake up this morning and not have the sleeping one there next to me. It wasn't even like I missed our morning talks, tho I suppose I might have if I had thought about it — it was more this sheerly physical thing, this place where my body is used to having her body, and now, just emptiness.

Meanwhile, here we are on the brink of that glorious beach known as Senior Spring, and it's forty-two degrees, and in English today Mic tells us we're going to be writing in-class essays every day for the next two weeks. That's so we can get ready for the AP. What fun. Haven't we had enough of these damn tests already?

Evidently not.

But that particular part of my future is bearing down on me, and way too fast — college notifications in April, and what about the summer? I don't know. I don't know anything. I don't even want to.

March 25th, 1980 *Tuesday*

Jesus. I am so nervous all the time over in Academy Hall! Always hiding, looking to see if Rik is coming, where can I jump if a head or arm attached to the rest of him appears. I feel like a coon in the corn and the dogs will be on me any time now.

Am I paranoid or what? 'Cause it's not like Rik is some thug or something. It's really me, I'm just so jumpy. I wonder if he's noticed I haven't called him yet. Oh god, I don't want to see him, I don't want him to know. He didn't really mean it — I'm too hypersensitive. But I still don't wanna anymore, that's for sure. No more, no more. But how would I even begin to explain it to him? I can't tell him, there's no way. He'll think I am such a baby. Or just a jerk.

March 27th, 1980 *Thursday*

So. I go to classes, slipping around like a little shadow. Today when Andrea touched me on the elbow outside of Econ, I think I jumped about three feet into the air.

She felt bad, that's for sure. Me, I felt like a stupid fool, a 'fraidy cat of the ninth degree, and maybe at the end of her ninth life too. I don't know, I can barely take this. It makes me so weird. Weird to myself, which I'm kind of used to, I guess, but weird to Andrea too, which I can hardly bear. What if she gets fed up with all my strangeness? It's hardly a way to act when your best friend taps you on the shoulder, rocketing up into space like the hounds were after you.

I am so weird. And really nervous. All the time. I just want to get the hell out of here. I can't take this.

March 28th, 1980 *Friday*

Mic called me over today after English. She'd handed us back our essays from Tuesday and Wednesday, and mine weren't so hot. She doesn't miss much, that Mic. She waited until the room had cleared, and asked me how I was doing. I was shifting my blue knapsack from one shoulder to the other, couldn't look at her. Well, if the quality of the essays was all she was worrying about — I don't think so, but she didn't pry exactly, just said she thought I looked tired a lot, my writing seemed scattered, how was I doing.

I went careening out of the top of my head right there. I told her yeah, I was tired, was feeling antsy these days to get out of Bristol, on to the next thing. She seemed to like that answer; she smiled and asked what next thing I was hoping for. I stumbled, said I didn't know, whatever, just as long as it was out of Bristol. Her smile slipped a touch; I think she started to see me then, how something is really wrong. God, it's true. I don't want her to see that tho! I can't let her see that!

Well. She said she could understand how I would feel that way, and then, lucky for me a few kids from her next class started wandering in. I looked over at them, Eliot Rutherford, for one, settling his long lanky form in a desk chair, and since, with those arrivals, Mic's moment was gone, I could get out of there. Which I did.

I wonder what she thinks. You don't suppose. . . .

No, I don't see how she could. But a couple of times in that vast new gym this afternoon, all of us on Williams' intramural softball messing around on one side, the girls' varsity lacrosse looping balls back and forth and hollering the other side of the massive net, I thought I saw Mic's face from far off scanning over at me thru the blue webbing. Maybe. Maybe.

I don't know. I don't know.

March 31st, 1980 *Monday*

What I can write about is Andrea — how I went to find her yesterday. She was in her room, thank god, sitting on her bed, sketching in that sketch book of hers. I must have looked a sight at her door; I don't know, but I know she saw my face and the way a hundred strands were coming undone from my braid and she got up from the bed, taking my hand and drawing me into the room, closing the door behind us.

First I sat on her bed, could barely speak, but

then I had to lie down. It was my back — I had to lie flat down. I wanted to howl, wanted to FREAK OUT, but you know I couldn't. Well, that's not exactly true, 'cause I did, but only a little, not much. I was making this funny noise 'cause I couldn't really breathe, and I buried my head in her pillow. God, keep me from crying! Andrea put her hands on my head, just rested them there. Finally I managed to swallow a full gulp of air. I asked her, mumbling into the pillow, if she would give me a back rub. Greedy huh?

So — she gave me maybe the best back rub I have ever had. She kept saying, "God, are you tight!" And she would work into one set of knots with her strong hands and then go to work further up or down on another spot, and when she worked back down to those first ones, they'd be all tight again. So tight that with her first touch back to them again, I'd flinch.

It was better after a while tho.

We didn't say anything much for a long time, but then, up out of nowhere, I heard myself saying, "So I, uh, I kind of had an argument with Rik."

I could feel her hands pausing for one teeny split half blink, and she said, "Hmm, an argument with Rik."

"Yeah," I said. Then a blank space and every possibility was shouldering its way into the small space of the room. I had to stop that swelling. I said, "Well, we are friends you know."

"Yeah, you used to hang out with him more in the fall."

I said that was true, I had. And then I had to close the thing some more.

"Yeah, well, I was over there, and we got into this thing, kind of an argument." God, I thought for sure it wasn't working, I didn't know how to cover, the whole top was going to come tearing off in the next second, no no no no, can not not not not do, I don't know how come I even write pieces of it in here. I know I shouldn't. Meanwhile I was lying there, and that reeling was starting in on me again, the fuzz taking over my head like algae choking a lake. We stopped talking, I didn't have to say anything more, one way or the other. And it was liké everything in her was going into her hands and right into my back — some way too how her hands working into me kept me from spinning away. Because God, how I spin away sometimes, into the ozone, lost in space.

So. We didn't go to dinner, she came with me to the snack bar later. She was so great — 'cause there I was, so tired, and spacey, and she didn't mind, just hung out with me, very even about all of it. She really is the best.

APRIL FOOLS DAY 1980 *Tuesday*

She's not gonna put up with me much longer, I don't think. Today I'm there with her, after ball, we're in a booth to ourselves at the snack bar and there was a blip, I don't know what; fuzz is all I know. And then all of a sudden Andrea's gripping my wrist, stopping this rapid tattooing I'm rapping on the table top with my spoon. It was like Snap! Wake up! Her eyes looking into mine, right in, "Stevie, hey Stevie, are you there?"

The thing was, I hadn't been at all. AT ALL. But I couldn't tell her that! I stared for a second, I don't know, like some little animal that's been stumbled over in the tall grass, the kind that looks up at you with glassy eyes, frozen. But I know her, I know her! Still, it don't matter, I'm slipping off anyway, and from that far, I can't even see here . . . . see her, I was going to say, but it's the same thing really now isn't it?

And yeah, I've always had this way of checking out I guess, kind of spacing away, bye-bye. I do it when I want to I guess, like if class is boring, poof! I'm gone! Other times too, when worse things were going on. No need for going into the details.

But now it's happening even when I don't want it to! Really bad! I'm gone before I even think about it, zip! Away! Shit, I must be crazy, this stuff sounds so crazy, floating off like that, I must be a psycho or something. I have to get a handle on this. At the rate I'm going they're going to lock me up someplace. Goddamn I don't know what to do. It must be time for bed tho. Maybe that's it: bedtime, sleep, eyes closed, don't think about it so goddamn hard because you make it worse. Maybe if you don't think about it at all, it will go away — ?

April 2nd, 1980 *Wednesday*

Oh god, I did it with her again today. What a fucked-up screwball I am. I'm too much of a flake, one minute I'm there with her, the next I'm gone.

I hate this. No — I hate me. I just can't get it together to work right. Never have. I think I'm just kind of broke. Actually I've known for a long time that that's my trouble. But now it's showing! I'm not being able to fake it anymore. Maybe *that's* why I'm checking out all the time these days.

April 4th, 1980 *Friday*

Maybe there's this way it bottoms out, and then heads back up again. Today I am better, the storm's somehow broken. Wish I could tell myself why. Yeah, that's me, always looking a gift horse in the mouth. The weight lifted, up went, when? This afternoon, somewhere in there, it was like I could taste my food again.

And then this evening I hung out with Andry and our two fine, fine friends. The after dinner coffee hour. L&D, they were asking me where I've been, but they didn't push it, so it was OK. Thank god. I was sitting there with them, feeling how much lighter my insides were. Tho if I'm going to keep myself honest here, I have to say I was feeling a little nervous too. My gut is still sort of like jello.

But anyway, there we were, the four of us, scrunched around a table for two, decaf in squat cups. The tables were re-painted over break and they are the brightest sort of fire engine red now. Something about the colors, our blank white cups, the relentlessly red table, the golden rod yellow bandanna in Andry's dark hair.

That's her. There's something about her . . .! Obviously! I don't think I know how to write it tho. So — meanwhile, Duncan is smoking. This is something I do know how to write about: the way Duncan smokes. She doesn't care what anybody says; you can tell by the way she holds her cigarettes to one side in her mouth. That girl is so cool she can't help it. She's always in jeans or black pants and she wears suspenders and vests and short-waisted army jackets, just this side of the dress code all the time. She's not another one of those loose-limbed golden-locked Westchester girls. The Admissions office would have never ever let her in, but she's Mr. Music Bob Duncan's daughter, so she gets to go here anyway. For free.

Anyway, as I was saying, we were sitting at that tiny blazing table. I was just glad to be there, feeling a bit of solid ground. Which — now that I think about it again — maybe started with English this morning, and actually that's what we were talking about mostly — English this morning, about Mic, how she let us have it for "outrageously stiff writing, death on paper." Well. Liddy was saying that she didn't know what Mic thought she could expect from us when we're writing AP essays, that of course we would write an essay for the AP differently than we would write an essay for Mic.

Liddy is funny — so airy and sharp both, especially when she's making a point, her hands flowing to emphasize the words that come out, edged with precision. Can't say I always agree with her, but is she ever smart.

Well, so, anyway, Liddy was saying how Mic is different than other teachers, because she wants our papers to have a lot of "I" in them. But the AP readers could care less about all us little I's, and so, of course, Liddy's argument goes, knowing that (and oh, we do, I agree with her there!), we're going to be more formal when they are our audience.

"Can't get away with all that indulgent I-ness," Liddy said, bending her willowy body over the table towards me. "C'mon Stevie, you were editor for The Rag, didn't you get fed up with all that first person stuff? I, I, I!! My god, such terribly earnest seriousness! Enough for a lifetime!"

Something I didn't like about her point. I turned towards Andrea, but she was keeping her mouth shut, looking to see what I would say, I think. I don't know, I thought Mic had been talking about something else. She's no dummy, and she doesn't think we are either. She's not looking for narcissistic blathering, she's trying to get at what it feels like to be ALIVE. Trying to get at the real. I tried to explain that to Liddy, well, explain it some, without giving too much of myself away. She didn't really buy it, I could tell. And meanwhile both Andrea and Duncan were sitting back, these half grins behind their coffee mugs, seeing, I suppose, how far we would take it.

Liddy doesn't have to agree with me tho. It's OK. What matters to me is that I walked into that classroom this morning not caring if I lived or died. It was that bad. Bad is the way it's been, but this morning I couldn't even fake my way thru, could barely work a half-ass smile up for Andrea, just sat there, and I was about to slip off for a class-long space odyssey when Mic dropped my essay on my desk. I looked up, and she was going around the room, not saying much, but I could feel the storm brewing in her. Usually that kind of thing scares me: uh-oh, now we've had it. But this morning I couldn't be bothered to be scared. Tho it did keep me on the planet, that's for sure.

So — Mic stepped back and exploded, cloudburst galore, thunder and lightning. But the thing was, it wasn't random or out of control, she was so fucking deliberate, I couldn't believe it. She didn't blow up in our faces, but all around us, over us, under us, the air charging and then changing, like the cleaning out of a thunderstorm. A good one.

"Where have you all gone to?!" Pacing thru the room, looking each one of us in the face as she walked, all thirteen of us. I looked right back at her, I had to, even from way back in where I was, I had to look out at her, meet that gaze as she went by, some moment of seeing — her into me, and strange, me seeing into her, somehow, and I saw something fierce, something too, almost a question, a searching I pulled up to and then fell back from, turning back in. That was enough for me!!

Once she got back up to the front of the room, she launched into us again, asking how it was that we had relapsed back into the conventional stiffness, why we had "returned to no-risk territory!" — exactly where she had started with us back in the fall. No one really said anything. I guess some of the kids were pissed, like Liddy, but me, I sat there, taking it in, something in me waking. And then she let it go for the meantime, and class went on. We got into a pretty good discussion of last night's reading. But I could tell Mic was still bugged. And I think I understand it.

"But Liddy," I was saying in the coffee room, leaning over the table myself, trying to keep my elbow out of the ashtray, "what about the 'inside' stuff, what she said about writing from *inside* your experience? Wearing your insides out? That's not necessarily the same thing as indulgent I-ness, it's about getting *real!*"

Liddy, however was not impressed. "Sounds great," she said wryly, "but will it get me a 5 on the AP?"

Finally it occurred to me that maybe Liddy and I were coming from places so far apart that we weren't going to find our common ground in one night over a red table. Getting real might get you a 5 on the AP, but then again it might not. I'm not sure a 5 on the AP ought to be the point in the first place. Because there's something else here that seems a hell of a lot BIGGER than that. It was there in Mic's eyes today, in that line of her mouth, the way she put her hand on her chest, smack, firm to the center, and said, "Write from here, write from here."

Isn't that sort of what I've been trying to do anyway, writing in this book? You know it is.

April 5th, 1980 *Sunday*

Here & Not-Here: A Play in 2 Voices

HERE: (silence)

NOT-HERE: That's right. Don't say it. Good girl.
Keep your mouth shut.

HERE: (silence)

NOT-HERE: Float away, float away, go away, go
away, away, away, away . . . . . .

HERE: Ummmmmm . . . . .

NOT-HERE: . . . into the wild blue yonder. . . .

HERE: . . . that face. . . !

NOT-HERE: Hey, c'mon! C'mon! Have you forgotten?
Space is the final frontier! C'mon and
space out with me!

HERE: That face, *her* face, will you lookit her?!!

NOT-HERE: What the fuck did I tell you? I thought
you knew better, you silly little fool!
Fuzz on you!

HERE: Oh . . . oh. . . .

NOT-HERE: Ohhh.. nothing! Fuzz on you! Fuzz
Fuzz Fuzz Fuzz! Fuzzy wuzzy izzy you!

HERE: I can't see, I can't see!

NOT-HERE: Fuzz, fuzz, that's what you get! My
god, thinking you want to see! Where
do you get off!

HERE: But I do want to see! I want to see
her face! Don't do this to me!

NOT-HERE: Now, now, sweetie, you *know* this is for
your own good!

HERE: Good? This doesn't feel good!

NOT-HERE: Oh, my little pumpkin, have you

	forgotten? There are things that feel worse than this! That's how we got here, remember? This is the way you wanted it!
HERE:	No way! Not me!
NOT-HERE:	Cut the back talk! Fuzz! Fuzz!
HERE:	No! No! I want to see her! Don't want to fuzz out anymore! Let me go! I *got* to see her!
NOT-HERE:	After all the fuzzing I've done for you! What an ingrate! Where would you have been, all these years without me! Me and my fuzz!
HERE:	I don't care! You got to let me go!
NOT-HERE:	Yeah? You don't know what you're talking about! You think you want to see? What about all that shit you don't want to see? What about all that? Don't tell me you don't know what I'm talking about, because you do!
HERE:	You're crazy! It's her I want to see!
NOT-HERE:	Haw! You think you get to pick and choose or something? Sorry, you sweet innocent! See one part, see it all!
HERE:	Oh god. Really?
NOT-HERE:	Uh-huh. You smarty pants. Sure you don't want some fuzz right this second? I can load it on, you know.
HERE:	(silence)
NOT-HERE:	Fuzzy wuzzy fuzzy izzy fuzzy always be!
HERE:	Andrea! Is that you!
NOT-HERE:	Forget her! It's not worth it!
HERE:	Andrea! Andrea!
NOT-HERE:	Fuzz! Fuzz! Fuzz?

87

HERE: Andrea! Andrea! I see you!

NOT-HERE: Fu ... All right! It's your fall! Don't come crying to me when it's more than you can handle!

April 6th, 1980 *Sunday*

My god. Did I really write that? Guess I did. Is this getting at it? Or is this losing it? The Fuzz. The Fuzz. Wraps me up, wraps me down. I do want to see her. I knew that before it popped into that crazy ass of a play I wrote last night. Yeah, and I guess I've known it for quite a while, haven't I? From that first time after Xmas break when I sat next to her on the bench in the locker room. I mean — that face! How else to put it?

But it doesn't matter when I start floating off. Well, nothing could matter enough, I can't help myself. It may be better these last couple of days, but who knows? God, it's awful the way I slip, falling away down into the morass of fuzz, gunky muzzling fuzzling stuff. Wall all around me I can't reach thru, I don't know how. But yesterday that stuff rushing thru my hand onto the paper, the NOT-HERE voice sneering, "Hey, that's the way you wanted it!"

Well??????????

So OK, maybe that's kind of true! But isn't everybody sort of like that? I mean there are always things in the world it'd be nicer not to see. Like babies starving in Bangladesh, kitties run over by tractors. Shit like that.

Yeah, but that's not the whole story either! I'm copping out here, I can feel it, there's more.

So. OK. There's this girl, right? She's back behind this wall. Can't see too good, that's for sure, things are kind of fuzzy, it's true, it's true.

So presto! She steps out — ? — and then — what? How the hell am I supposed to know! All right all right, just pretend then. OK, here goes. She steps out and suddenly she's out in the middle of the whole world. What does she see then? It's not just the starving babies or smooshed kitties that's the problem, is it?

All right, all right, there's other shit I don't want to see, I admit it, stuff now, stuff before. Like that fucker Philip for one. Yuk! I dunno. Maybe my eyes aren't strong enough to take all this seeing. Haw! That's why I wear contacts, right? But no, I got to see Andrea. I do.

Is that the bottom line then? Really? Yes, yes, it is. Her I got to see. What ever it takes.

So. OK. What if we start out with sneak peeks? Then turn away when it's been enough for a day? What about you try a little at a time, OK?

OK.

April 8th, 1980 *Tuesday*

We compared AP notes after dinner tonight, over decafs. Well, me over a Coke, the others with their white cups. I had them laughing — me! That's usually Andrea's job, but I was wound for sound, as they say. Myself, can't say I understood where it came from, but at least there was no fuzzing today in this district! the outrageous burning clear thru, bouncing hard with an edge.

I went into that AP this morning with that edge honed. Walked into the Lecture Hall, cavernous dark green pit of a school room, and when I sat down, I knew I was going to write exactly whatever I thought, no bullshit at all. Straight from that HERE place.

I sat down and the thing began. I chose the question about characterization. Fine. How does characterization work to inform the point of view in fiction. Cite from two works. I decided on Moby Dick and Lear. Fine. But I didn't really know where I wanted to go with any of it yet. The thing is I usually plan all this stuff out in advance when I'm taking a test, ponder and make an outline, the whole formal process. But this morning, no. This morning I just wrote!

I wrote that these two books portrayed dictatorial types way too kindly, took too many pains to show how the oh-so-tragic flaws of their beings drove them to their horrible endings, as if once we could all be made to understand that, then we would, perforce, pity them, not hold them responsible. I wrote, in so many words, that that was garbage, and could never excuse them of the crime of dragging so many down with them. I said these characterizations served to inform the point of view of the authors who wanted to get these "great" guys off the hook. But what about John Doe? That's what I wrote. How come what he's thinking and feeling isn't worthy of note?

I bet they won't like me writing that. But I don't care what I get anymore. I'm so tired of bullshitting. I'm just too horsed off to do it anymore. Fuck it. If I can't write what I really care about, and if I can't write the truth about it, I won't write at all. Otherwise what am I doing here anyway?

What am I doing here anyway? Not fuzzing out, that's for sure. Not today anyway. Probably 'cause I was too cranky for there to be any room left over for fuzz.

Huh. Now isn't that interesting.

April 9th, 1980 *Wednesday*

Spring sure is a season in this part of the world. Not like Vermont where winter clenches its frigid teeth, hangs on right into the bitter dregs of late April, and then — pop! — it's all of a sudden summer full-blown. Spring here is definitely a transition from one state of things to the next.

Weird things happened today. It'd be easier, really, to write more about the weather, an in-depth philosophy of the season perhaps.

But no. I was with Andrea today. Andrea, Andrea, Andrea. Andrea Snyder. Stevie (Stephanie really, yak) Roughgarden. Together on a sunny spring day. It was Andrea's idea. Not that I objected or anything, tho I was worried I might get weird.

Well. We rode on our bikes the ten miles out to Humpback, hiked an hour up to the lookout, threw ourselves sweating and tired on that enormous flat top rock, looking out, looking up, looking all around.

The view from Humpback is tremendous — you can see all of the town and the lake too, and over towards the horizon you can see where Bradfield starts, the edge of the city. Like that — expansion — I can take. Give me the horizon. But then all of a sudden we were looking at each other, up close close close! and her eyes are teal, the color darker in a circle around the outside, lighter and lighter further in.

I felt it. I felt it in my arms, her eyes in my arms. God, I am so weird. I don't want her to think the wrong thing, and she doesn't, not yet, I don't think, 'cause she wouldn't look back at me so steady and calm if she did.

I fuzzed. I looked, she looked, I looked, and I fuzzed. AGGGH! Like a piece of lint swooped up in breeze, wafted off towards the horizon. I looked down, could feel the reeling starting. Needed something, some little anything to pull myself back towards the world with, spied one of those little helicopter seeds all weatherbeaten and grey lying on the ground. I snatched it up, staring at it intently, the tiny ragged tears coming and going, clear, and foggy again thru the thickening. Aggh. I started shredding it, millimeter by millimeter, hey *this* one ain't gonna fly off no more! And suddenly her hand was on my hand and my insides jerked and I looked up.

She was looking — really looking! even further in than before — right at me. She's intense! And it was like I was a kite torn away that she was re-mooring — her eyes were the place to land. Oh god, that's not quite it even yet. It was like she reached across the light years of outer space and found me in a place where no one's ever seen to in me, and without saying a word, waved me back to the world.

I couldn't believe it. I turned half towards her, not believing it, but it was happening, her face so calm, her eyes on mine. I looked back, looked back, looked back.

"How'd you do that?" I finally found the words.

She said, "What?"

"That!"

"What, how did I look at you? Easy! I like to!"

Oh zing! How could I tell her how much I like looking at her? I couldn't. I know it means something different for me than it could possibly mean to her. I mean, she's an artist! She's supposed to look at things!

I ducked the point, went on, saying, "I was off in Fuzzland, and you reached right in! Right in thru all the fuzz and the wall!"

"Fuzzland?" She didn't know what I was talking about. Why would she? So I explained it to her, if such a thing is possible, which it isn't really, all you can say is, well, it's *like* this, it's *like* that, but she seemed to get it for the most part anyway. I asked her if she thought I was some kind of freak, and she said no way. God I hope she's not saying that just to be nice. I don't think she was tho.

Then we were lying there, side by side, resting, the sun lying flush on top of us, warming everything, and no, I didn't fuzz out. I was there all right. Kind of wish I hadn't been.

I am so weird! How could I feel this way! I got to stop. Maybe it's better to be off in Fuzzland after all. But no, you can't say that. Just say that you got to think about something else next time. Next time, next time. Oh god, I'm even feeling it now, what to do about that? Not the fuzzing, but the fizzfizzfizzing! It's back. I thought you got over that, Stevie. What's wrong with you anyway? I think all your years of being bedded down have perverted you! You are really some kind of sickie to think about your friend that way!

Oh, but c'mon, I didn't really want to do anything up there on the mountain! Just wanted to, wanted to — WRITE IT! wanted to turn and snuggle up close to her side. But I can't! I have to keep my greedy little thoughts to myself. I can't let her know, no way. She'd hate me, I know it. Got to hang in here now; I'll be out of this place soon enough, and when I get to college next year, I'll start over, maybe grow up and get normal already.

April 10th, 1980 *Thursday*

ILOVEHER ILOVE HER I LOVE HER!

And no one ever has to know 'cept me.
It's OK if I just keep it to myself.

Today we hung out in her room after lunch, talking, not talking. She played her guitar for a while. She's been working on this new song, and I begged her to play it for me. Finally she gave in. She apologized all over the place before she played it tho, saying it wasn't finished, it was still rough. I don't know what she was apologizing for. It was a great song, good tune and good words, stuff about a new season and a new start.

New, new. I know she must be thinking about next year, moving on to a new life in college. Which is nice and all, but I felt really sad thinking about it, listening to her play. I am really going to miss her next year.

But I don't have time to think about that right now. Have to get to the English assignment. Some essay about women in literature. That's what I should be doing here, reading English. But all I really want to do is write about Andrea! God, I think I am really sunk! Because I do like her, I really do! It's Love, yeah, this incredible fondness. I see her, and it's right there, swelling up in me, and my eyes want to swallow her whole.

Jesus Stevie! You're a girl! Have you forgotten!!! Girls are not supposed to feel this way about *girls*!!!

All right, all right, don't sweat it, it's just a couple of months more, and we're out of here, go to Harvard and grow up. It's just a phase, you'll stop thinking about her then. You'll have to! As for now, just get to work. Work. Work.

*April 11th, 1980 *Friday**

I can't believe it! That essay Mic had us read for today, it talked about — about — well, it was called "Voices Silenced." This good friend of Mic's, Susan somebody, wrote it as part of her Phd thesis. She's really something, I'll tell you that! I've never read

stuff like what she's saying before. Really incredible
stuff, about how almost all of the so-called great
books have been written by white men, how women's
voices have not been heard — white women's voices,
black women's voices, and — aggggh! — even lesbian
voices! Did I just write that? I think I did. This
woman Susan did too. She really did. She talked
about a lot of things in that essay, but she talked
about lesbians too. Lesbians!!!!!! Jesus.

She mentioned this one writer in particular, Rita
Mae Brown. Rita Mae Brown wrote a book called
"Rubyfruit Jungle." It's a lesbian book! I didn't know
you could write a book about being a lesbian. I
guess you can tho.

God, I can't believe Mic gave us this essay to
read. But she's really into it, that's for sure. Well,
she didn't really talk about the lesbian part, but she
talked about a lot of the different books Susan
mentioned, sounds like she has most of them, she's
such a book hound anyway. I've been in her
apartment and they're all over the place, and not
only on the shelves. Books sit around her place like
pets, on the table, on the counters, all over the floor.
But I bet she doesn't have that Rubyfruit one.

God, I got to write about something else. How
about the weather? Things are warming up all
around here I'd say. This afternoon out on the field
we were most of us stripped down to T shirts. It
was great, the sun blazing over our heads. Every
year the first hot day always makes me wonder, oh
god, am I going to be able to take the heat? This
year I think, no problem. Life is more fun in T

shirts anyway. And Andrea looked so good today, I could barely take it. She is so cute! Out there in cut off army pants and the black T cut off at the shoulders. Oh god, her shoulders! Jesus, here I go again. Jesus, Jesus, Jesus!

Help me!

April 13th, 1980 *Sunday*

Oh god, I am really in the grip of something here. Oh god. Woke up with this feeling of having been washed thru and filled with something. With her. All night long, I was thinking, not thinking really, not quite dreaming either, stuff about Andrea's new song, new starts; her songs all out in the world, in a box and in the ground, and we're trying to get them out, and her guitar is everywhere, I have to help her get it out of trees and from barns and out back in this field.

Andrea, Andrea, and me, now here alone in my bed, waking at dawn, first weak strips of light over the trees that clump along the other side of the fairway, and it's like she's coming out my pores, like I've soaked her in, me the sponge, and I'm filled with her, right down to my gut, I can't help it, she's just IN there, so much so that the overflow is seeping out of me, ringing the air all around me.

God, what am I going to do?
Maybe if I could read that Rubyfruit book, I could let off a little steam . . . . . ?

April 14th, 1980 *Monday*

RUBYFRUIT REVELATION!

This book is so fucking great! It is the best book
I have ever read! She really writes it! She really
does! God! I can't believe it! But I do! I have to!
Because it's right there! Why didn't anyone ever tell
me about this book before!!! Oh, but I know why, it's
'cause Molly is so proud and nobody in the world is
going to stop her and who wants to go putting those
ideas into the kids' heads!

This woman is so into it, no apologies. I didn't
know you could do that. But she does! She's someone
who knows what she wants and goes for it. And
what she wants is women. Just like the way I want
Andrea, it's true. Yes, it is indeed true.

Oh god.

But it's OK to feel that way after all I guess.
And I do feel better — thanks to Rita Mae. And Mic.
She was so cool yesterday when I showed up at her
door. She invited me in, gave me some Coke. We sat
on the rug and talked about how class is going. I
told her how much I like the essay her friend Susan
wrote. I told her I think Susan must be brilliant.
She smiled, said maybe I was right. God, I was so
nervous! Because I had a plan, see, but I wasn't
sure I had the nerve. But I just kept talking, said
how I wanted to read some of the books Susan
mentions. Then — I did it! I asked her if she had
any of them. She said she did. All of them tho? She
thought actually she did. My heart was fully in my
mouth with that! Kind of made it hard to talk. But
I said how I wanted to do some outside reading,
maybe I could take a look thru them?

Mic got right up and showed me the shelf. The one over by the window. I got up behind her, and scanned the titles. But it wasn't there! I must have checked five times, but it really wasn't!

So. I could walk out with books I didn't really want to read. Or I could ask for the one I really wanted. I took a deep breath. Mic was back in her chair. I turned towards her. Said, "I thought you said you had all of them, Mic?" My voice sounded small to me.

What was she thinking then? I don't know. She paused, gave me this flash of a funny look I couldn't quite make out. I didn't know what to do. God, what does she think!! But it was too late. I said, "What about that Rubyfruit one? I — uh — want to read something a little off the beaten track."

She stood up kind of fast, saying she did have it. This flash went thru me — hope and fear both. Jesus, I'm sometimes way too much, even for myself. But I'm so glad I asked! Mic glided by me on her bare feet, headed down the hall, saying she'd get it. I couldn't sit tho. I followed, just nosey I guess, trailed behind her to the doorway of her room. Her room is even cooler than the rest of the place! She has her bed on the floor, just like Andrea! More books all over, of course, but a really cool red and purple bedspread and pictures on the wall of all her friends and in one corner a candle in a holder on a scarf.

Mic was in the closet, bending over some boxes, going, "Hmmm, I know it's in here someplace." I guess she has so many books that she has to keep some of them in there! She was talking to me, her voice muffled, "Just hold on here, I know I have it someplace." I laughed 'cause I didn't know what else to do, plus I was so bloody nervous still. So I was just looking around her room some more. There was this nice photo I liked on the little table next to her bed, framed — Mic and some woman, smiling and sort of squinting too, 'cause they're looking into the sun. The other woman has her arm slung over Mic's shoulder and the shadow of the person taking the shot is stretching out on the ground towards them. They look happy. Maybe it's her sister. I was standing there, thinking about how I wish I had a sister, when Mic called out, "Eureka!" She emerged from the boxes holding up *the* book.

Which she gave to me! She really did! I took it, and right away started talking about something else, about this game last week we played in intramural softball which was particularly fun. We walked back down the hall towards the living room, but the door is down that way too, so I saw my chance and took it. I was out of there! Thanking Mic as I went, making no special mention of the book's topic — of course.

But god, she must suspect! How could she not! All right so maybe she does. But maybe with a friend like Susan who writes about this kind of stuff in an essay for her Phd, maybe with a friend like that, Mic might be pretty liberal herself. She can't think it's all that bad if she went to the trouble of buying the book, right? Mic is pretty cool, after all. And she didn't have to lend it to me either! But she did.

HOORAH HOORAH HOORAH!

April 15th, 1980 *Tuesday*

EVERYTHING ELSE ASIDE!

I was starting to wonder why I hadn't heard from any schools yet. But it's the old bus stop trick, wait and wait and nothing comes, until when finally it seems there can be no hope, the flood descends upon you. Three today: UVM yes, but of course, and Williams yes, won't Pops be pleased and Hampshire yes, but he won't like that.

Nothing from Harvard. I don't think anyone has heard from Harvard yet tho. So I shouldn't worry on that score.

What if I don't get in?

What if I do?

Yeah, well, worry about that when the time comes, how about it?

I finished Rubyfruit last night. I was going back to bed, 'cause I wrote for so long and it was late. But I thought, OK, well just ten pages then. But no way. I went at it and got pulled along until there I was, at the end and it was two o'clock.

God, what a great, great book. Who cares about colleges anyway? Just live!

April 16th, 1980 *Wednesday*

God! Goddamn goddamn goddam! I am in the deep shit now. He is going to kill me, I know it. God, I should have studied harder last semester. But

I didn't, and now it's like everything he said is proven out. He is going to KILL KILL KILL KILL me!

Shit shit shit shit!

Got the letter this afternoon. Last class of the day is over, lunch behind me, Andry's not around. I walked down to the PO, saw the one long thin envelope in the box. Fumbled with the dial, drew it out, and sure enough, there it was: Harvard Admissions, and the thing was so skinny I knew right away that it looked bad. I stared down at that blank white envelope. How come one stupid little piece of paper, something you hold so lightly in your hand can have such a big impact on your goddamn life?

Well, I couldn't stand there all day. I opened it, and read the opening, "We regret to inform you. . . ." I couldn't read it thru. Not till later anyway. I hurled it away from me, but of course, being paper, it didn't go very far.

Couldn't feel anything much, but I knew, I *know* what's coming. Walked back here and I haven't shown my face since. Dad didn't call. Thank god. He will, tho, I know. And what am I going to say?

I don't want to go to Williams! A few months ago it seemed like a good second choice, but now I think about it and it feels like it would be so much more Bristol, nothing much different, just a little bigger, same kind of preppy people, preppy ways, preppy attitudes, Izod shirts and corduroy. Maybe I am too proud, like Dad says, but I don't know if I can take four more years of this shit. Hell, I know I can't! But how do I tell *him* that?

April 17th, 1980 *Thursday*

Well . . . . the note's still on the door. I wasn't around earlier for the call, I stayed away. On purpose of course.

I kind of lost my shit at breakfast. Andrea came up, setting down her tray and I was looking down into my cereal bowl. But I couldn't hide my face forever. When she saw my look, she said right away, "What's wrong?!"

I told her. "Harvard turned me down."

"Those assholes!" She sat down next to me, put her arm around me. "You pretty bummed?"

I was nodding, got out some version of the fact that my father is going to kill me, but then I could feel the tears seizing my throat and I couldn't talk. She brought me closer. Jesus, I could have just fallen apart into my Captain Crunch, I could feel it, this whole ocean wanting to wash over and drown me. Tons and tons of tears, whole seas, stormy ones. But shit! Not at breakfast! I mean, really! I pulled myself together. I had to. And we didn't say anything, either one of us, for a while, and then it was time for class.

We stood up, and she asked me if I was all right, and I nodded. 'Cause I was, mostly anyway. She threw her arms around me, and held me, and she was the warmest thing ever in my life!!

That's what I was wishing for tonight, again, the warmest thing ever in my life.

We were in her room, studying. Well, I wasn't really, tho I was trying, reading French sort of, but having a hard time sticking with it. Ça va? I was sitting at the desk, feet up, she was stretched out on

103

the bed, reading Spanish, one arm over her head, looking rumpled and sleepy. When I had to go back for check-in, she was still lying there like that. Me, I stood in her doorway, looking back, wanting so bad to walk back in and curl in next to her, hold her close to me!!! Oh god. And be held! Oh more god!!

That's enough for tonight!

April 18th, 1980 *Friday*

I just got off the phone with him, and my nerves are still so jangled, rubbed raw, bleeding inside. So I didn't get into Harvard! Why is that the end of the world! What a tirade! Blasted down over my head. He was shouting at me over the phone, all about how I am slipping, getting lazy, I should have worked harder last semester, don't I think about my future, he knew things were taking a turn for the worse when I quit the hockey team.

"Life is hard, you know Stevie," he said, over and over. He says that a lot, and I hate it. Cuz what about my life? MY LIFE? My ever-loving LIFE? Oh god, I think I am going to suffocate — the way the throat closes in.

April 20th, 1980 *Sunday*

It's midnite, and I just got back from Andry's. I have to write about this!

We were hanging out in her room, both of us

reading, and out of the blue, *she* said, "Hey, let's swap back rubs, what do you say?"

How do I write about this? I love touching her! Is that so bad? I didn't do anything except give her a massage! But god, what if she knew? You'd think the charge in my fingers alone would tip her off, call the big booming truth out to her. I don't know what she knows. I think things are getting a little bit thick around here. I mean I wasn't about to start anything funny, but I don't know how much of this up close stuff I can take. I mean, I would never do anything! I'm not like that! But jesus! The fizzing was so bad it was about to erupt out of my ears like a Coke bottle shook up just before you pop the cap.

And then she gave me a massage. It was great. Just her touching me is heaven enough! But she's really good with her hands too, knows how to get into the places that are sore. It's like she can smell them and goes right for them. I don't have to say a word. She just knows. Oh, oh, oh. It was great, but it was sort of like a long tickle too. The charge still building. I-yi. How much of this can I take?

When she was done, she just sort of let her hands lie on my back. Neither of us saying anything for a while, me still soaking in the feel of her, not wanting to budge. She said something about her dad, about missing him. I said, "What?"

And she started talking about him in earnest. I turned on my side and listened, watching her face. I even got it together to ask her a few questions. It was good. I think sometimes me and Andry act like I'm the one with all the problems. 'Course I don't talk about them much, but still it seems like the understanding between us is that's how it is. It's too much like I'm the kid, and she's always got to be watching out for me. That's not fair to her. Hell, but it's not fair to me either! I can't keep being the kid in these things my whole life! You know? I'll never grow up!

So I was listening hard — I am a good listener — and asking her questions, and trying to point out stuff in what she said. After a while, she got quiet, and then! Then she kind of slid down on the bed and was next to me, lying there, not saying anything, breathing slow. And just when I thought maybe she was going to cry, she snuggled up close to me! I felt seized — jesus, what am I supposed to do?! 'Cause I was feeling for her, but I didn't want her to think I was feeling too much, you know? But, even worse, I didn't want her to think I wasn't feeling at all!

So. I half put my arm around her, and ran my hand thru that wonderful thick head of dark curls, hoping my hand could say all the things I could not. The love stuff, that is, not the other stuff. Andry didn't say anything, moved in yet closer to me. I could feel how sad she was. It didn't show when she was talking of course, but with her body so close to mine, I could feel it in her, this sharp welling up in her. Beyond words.

Ten minutes? Fifteen? It was forever, it was no time at all. Then they were coming around for check-in, we could hear them, and right away we both moved at the same time to get up. Oh god, god, I didn't want to! But it wouldn't be cool if Susy poked her head in on that sight! She wouldn't understand. I mean, it would look funny. Damn it, damn it! Why couldn't we have started in on that after check-in? Maybe we could have fallen asleep that way! Not that I would fall asleep how I was feeling, but maybe she would! And I could hold her. That would make me so happy!

God, would she like that? Oh god Stevie, shut up! Don't go looking to take advantage of a situation! Just because she wants some comfort doesn't mean anything more than exactly that! And I am glad I could give her some. Because it was somehow something more. I mean, I felt strangely older, something about having something so — what? — important, precious, entrusted to my holding, even if only for ten minutes.

Maybe that's what love is: holding something precious.

April 21st, 1980 *Monday*

First day of the English mini-courses, and I think this is going to be the best class I have ever been in. We are going to write, really write. Get at IT. And the people in the class are cool. The right sort for such a project. There's Ken and Duncan, and Val and Sylvie and Eliot. And me. Not so sure about Eliot tho; he's always struck me as the snide sort. But we'll see. If he's not cool, there's enough of the rest of us so maybe we can keep him in line.

Anyway — it was a great class today; Mic had us write about what writing means to us, why it matters to us. I wrote something about trying to be aware, trying to be more fully alive. Of course that bit about being alive, I kind of got from Mic herself, that stuff she says about writing from the inside, wearing your inside out.

I've learned so much from her. Hope now I can learn even more.

April 22nd, 1980 *Tuesday*

I went over to Andrea's room last night. With no excuse at all, just had to see her. I tapped at her door and heard her soft "come in!" She was sitting on her bed, quietly strumming her guitar. She had her pajama pants on and her big old green sweatshirt, and she was so beautiful to me! She looked up and gave me the biggest and most wonderful smile, this piece of surprise underlining it. I don't usually bop by after check-in. You're not even supposed to go off your floor after eleven, and I'm the type who gets very nervous about getting caught. But last night I didn't care.

Next thing I knew we were sitting on her bed together, side by side, with our backs against the wall, oh heaven. Andrea asked me if I've made up my mind yet about schools, and all I could say was that I don't know. I guess I'm putting it off. I figure I have until the end of the week anyway. And besides I didn't want to talk about that. I started telling her about how great I think Mic's class is, how I think it's going to be all about writing about the way things really feel. We got into this really great conversation about how art works to express stuff — Andrea was saying how she can say things with her sculpture that she can't say any other way. We went on and on.

Then! Right around the point it felt to me like we were both talked out, she said she was tired and put her head on my shoulder. My insides leaped up, ohmigod! Well. I wasn't going to be no stone, so I put one hand on her head, ran my hand thru her hair. Just like Sunday night, and it felt as good, I can tell you that. Oh oh oh!

Just like that, for ten minutes. That and nothing more. Not me to move on her. Not me. I mean, she trusts me, and I would never, never. So when the fizzfizz started getting to me, I mean, MY GOD FIZZ! I said I had to go do a little history. She made a kind of 'aw' noise. Maybe I should have stayed. But I couldn't! I mean, I was getting these impulses, oh god, these impulses. And hell, after reading Rita, there's no way I can't see those for what they are.

That's just the way it is — the way I am.

April 23d, 1980 *Wednesday*

Me, I hung out in my room this afternoon, trying to read, and Andrea was up in the art room, doing her thing. I missed her, I have to say, had this ache in me to see her. But I don't know, I don't know. I'm not sure I can stand it, how I get feeling when I am with her. Maybe a little time off is good.

April 25th, 1980 *Friday*

Shit. I don't know what I'm going to do with myself the rest of the term. I just wanna, wanna, wanna! Arggh! Teeth grinding.

Out of it all day, but then this, we meet up walking back to the dorm ten minutes before check-in.

So. We're standing there off the path, under the ginkgo, the shadows of the trees scatting around from the lamplight, the light and dark dancing on your face. I wanted so much to draw you into my arms and hold you, touch your face — softly! — with a single finger.

Good god! Not only that!
I wanted to kiss her!
Bad!

She was looking at me with something in her eyes —

what? — and it was like something inside me jumped only one split second before I would have been totally taken with this tide that was building and building in me. I swift moved my arm and looked at my watch and we had half a minute before check-in.

So we ran. Hard. She beat me to the door, but then I went past her on the stairs. When we got to my landing, I just ducked off and said, "See you!"

God, I hope that wasn't rude! But it was too close of a call. Too close all around I think. I-yi, what the fuck am I gonna do?!

And what about the look on her face in that silent moment we held still — something soft, some piece of a question? ??? Oh god, next thing you know, I'm going to be making things up in my head! It's not possible, I know it's not, so don't torture me with it!

April 27th, 1980 *Sunday*

I just got off the phone with Dad. I don't know if I can write anything.

But I'm thinking — maybe I could hack it for another four years. At a Bristol kind of place I mean. It's not *that* bad, is it? Plus I know how to deal with it. I really do. And the Williams campus is pretty and there's an Outing Club too.

Maybe he's right — maybe Hampshire would be too flaky. Probably they let you get by there because that's the groovy thing. I don't care about being a great lawyer or having the "right" diploma, but I do care about learning. I don't want to go someplace where they're just flaking everything off. You can tell that at Williams they expect a lot — you got to perform and everything. So I would definitely learn a lot there.

Maybe he's right. Maybe it would be a big mistake to go to Hampshire. I wasn't thinking that way this morning, but he made a good case for Williams. When he's not yelling at me, my old man can talk good sense.

April 29th, 1980 *Tuesday*

Oh shit. I want to put the whole thing off. I know I should go to Williams. I know it's the sensible thing. I know I should have called them this morning. I have got to call them tomorrow. Period. Because shit it's already crazy late. I don't think there's anybody else who is still hanging fire with their decision. Just weird old me.

Maybe Williams wouldn't be that bad. Maybe I could cut it there.

But oh jesus, I remember how I felt when I visited that place, like I would never be able to breathe there. And the first thing I saw that rainy afternoon when we pulled in, that massive wave of yellow slickers advancing over the hill, a hundred hundred students, all in identical preppy rain wear, tromping across the lawn. A great yellow tide! Yagh, I'll drown!

Still! Maybe I'm just making too big a deal of it. Maybe I'm just overreacting.

I just don't know. I just don't know!!
HELP!!!!!!!

April 30th, 1980 *Wednesday*

Holy cow, I'm going to Hampshire!!!!!

An astounding sequence of events, ladies and gentlemen, led to this sudden and dramatic decision!

I'm going to Hampshire, I'm going to Hampshire!

Practically next door to Andrea too! Well, not exactly, but damn close. Damn close.

Holy shit, I can't believe it.

112

But it is exactly the thing I've wanted to do. I just couldn't say it to myself, much less wish it for myself. Thank god for running into Mic out on the playing fields this afternoon — literally, that is. We were both out on runs. I still hadn't made any calls, which is pretty outrageous. If I had managed to pull that stunt for much longer, I wouldn't have been going to any school at all!

But we met up out jogging, and so there we were, trotting along together, and she called over to me, "So where you going, Stevie?"

"Back to the dorm after this," I quipped. Very clever, huh?

"You know what I mean! Where are you going?"

"I don't know!"

"Where you want to go?" We were rounding the far corner. I didn't answer, scrunched up my face. She repeated the question, put emphasis on each word as she said it. "Where you want to go?" With the most weight on the word "want."

"Hampshire," I said. It just popped out, like that. I surprised myself!

"So you going to Hampshire, Stevie?"

"I don't know!" We were running pretty hard and I could feel my lungs stretching, feel the swelling of the pain. But there was this power in it too, the way we swung along, even fast stride side by side. We ran and ran, and then, with the last wide stretch of green before us, we took one look at each other, and broke into this sprint! Pounding furiously, running flat out, the flight in our bodies, the sun in our eyes. Something about our bodies coursing along together, some rhythm in our running. Something about together. All the way to Adams like that.

Afterwards we were both bent over in that post-run body bend. And when we straightened, we looked at each other again, and we just started laughing. I can't even say about what exactly, just something in the way it felt, something we knew without saying, even.

So. We stood there for a bit, just sort of stretching, not saying anything much. Then Mic said she had to go. She had one leg up on the railing that runs along way down to the basement there. She fixed me with a look.

"Stevie!" she said. She brought her leg down and stood tall up.

For a moment she scared me with that urgency in her voice. "What?" I said back.

"Go the way your blood beats Stevie."

"My blood beats?" I echoed her.

"Yeah, go the way your blood beats. That's the only thing I know to tell you. The rest is up to you." She was turning to go. "And oh yeah — good luck. See you in class!" She walked into the dorm. Just like that. I heard the door close behind her, and I heard her words going round in my head, and I thought of the way my blood had just been beating in me right then as she and I thudded across the green, and I thought about the way it felt right, and I thought about the way sometimes some things just do feel right. Even when you can't explain them.

Well. I ran back to my dorm. All I can say is that Dad was not pleased when I called him. He blew up actually. I almost lost my resolve. But I just hung on. Clenched the receiver in my still-sweaty hands and stuck to it. Thru all his ranting about how I don't know what I'm doing, I'm ruining my life, how I could

114

have just gone to the lousy union high school back in Vermont if this was what I was going to do.

I didn't argue. But I didn't budge either. That's pretty good for me. And I know I can get away with it too; I know he'll pay for Hampshire because he hates the thought of me falling all together off the college track worse than he hates the idea of me at Hampshire. With all "those flakes, bleeding hearts and queers!" as he put it.

Jesus, if he only knew the things I think about! But I don't have to tell him anything.

It is my life, isn't it? And my education. That's how it's going to be at Hampshire. MY education. If I want to learn a lot, I can. It's my responsibility. And it will be what I want to learn, not what some old ivy-covered man thinks I should know.

*May 1st, 1980 *Friday**

MAYDAY MAYDAY!

Where the hell has Andrea gone to? I know I haven't been around much myself, that I was sort of hiding out last week, but shit, she's never around anymore. She didn't even come to ball today. I did see her for a minute after class — I just had to give her my news about Hampshire. And yeah, she looked happy to hear it, but then she took off anyway. For the art studio of course.

Is she avoiding me? Or am I just getting paranoid?

May 2nd, 1980 *Saturday*

Jesus, she takes off right after dinner! Just takes off! With a little wave and "I'm going to the studio, now, bye," and that's that! Jesus! I haven't seen her for days, and what am I supposed to do for fun tonight? What is her fucking problem anyway? Does she think I'm going to just wait around until she's ready to come out of her garret someday to rejoin the human race? Is this some kind of test or what?!

I AM SO RIPSHIT!
$#*!@#$%!!?

(FREAK OUT TIME OUT)

May 3d, 1980 *Sunday*

!!!!!

*May 4th, 1980 *Monday*

Hear ye, hear ye!

At brunch yesterday morning for an hour and a half and no Andry — where is she? Where, Where, Where!!!!!! Something in me cracked, split wide open all arms and heart and run and find her. So I did. She was up there in that sky blue studio, seated on a stool and bent over the wide table in the art studio — her purple shirted back to the door. Heart, stomach, and entire intestines in my throat, I pushed the door open and she turned around, just glancing at first, then saw it was me and stuck there, half twisted atop her seat. I didn't know what to say. I was beside myself, struck mute. Finally I said, "Hi."

She said, "Hi." It was obvious we both knew with the rush of air I had brought in that something was up. Very awkward. Andry shifted her weight on the stool. The silence was getting thick.

I couldn't take it. I asked, "So where you been?" How about that for getting to the point! Andrea gestured around the room, long fingers making a sweep, red kerchief headband so bright against her dark curls it seemed to flash. My eyes followed the arc of her hand. I started talking off the top of my head, something about how much work she must be getting done. She was already nodding, and started to launch into this whole thing about it, talking about this piece, that piece. I know I should be interested in her art, and usually I am, but I could feel some part in me beginning to break off, like I was going to go away, fuzz out. I made a grab for

117

myself, reaching for her with it, blurting, "I miss you Andry!"

She stopped short, looked down at the floor like she was embarrassed. The silence swelling again and I wanted to splash turpentine into the dense hole between us, set it afire and jump in, blazing, blazing. But the blazing was inside me, too much now, the explosion of it, and up out of it I was asking Andrea all in a tumble of words if I'd done something wrong, was she mad at me, was she tired of me, something, anything, what?

Right away she was shaking her head hard, saying over and over, "No, it's not you, it's me. It's me." Protesting that of course she'd never tire of me, how could I think that?

How could I? But I did. I suppose some part of me still does. Deep down I'm not sure anybody sticks around much longer than your average barn cat, if you know what I mean.

But all the while I was looking at her. How I've come to relish her looks! Her fine features and that curly black head of hair and the crook in her left ear and the line of her collar bone just under her shirt when it hangs open. The way she talks with her hands, how her eyebrows slant and dive with the words. And her eyes. Those eyes. How many more times could I have sat there like that, drinking in her being but not saying the words?

"I love you!"

She looked up, fast, sharp. My heart cried out, wanted to hide, but I looked right back at her. And then, the words coming quiet out of her, "I love you too." Oh! The wild hope reeling up in me! I have to confess right here and now that I have been hoping all along; it's been this little, wild voice deep down under. But still there's this other voice in me too. Always it says, "It's too good to be true! Don't even bother hoping, it won't happen! It's too good to be true!"

But this time I ran out ahead of that voice, and the words were past my lips before I could even change my mind. "But I *really* love you Andrea." Oh gulp, here was coming everything or nothing.

"Yeah?" Her head was bent but I could see one long thin eyebrow go up.

"Yeah. REALLY. You can tell me I'm a freak if you want to, but it's true."

"A freak?" She would hardly look at me.

"Yeah — I mean I don't know what you think about that kind of stuff. But if it — uh — flips you out, I'll understand."

"What kind of stuff are you talking about? Like what kind?"

"That kind of love!" I said, feeling foolish. And terrified. What if —? Oh what the hell, just say it, the damage was already done. I threw one hand out. "You know — love — love like Romeo and Juliet, but you're not a boy!" Part of me was screaming at the rest to shut up. But it was too late!

"And you're not a boy either," Andrea said slowly, in a matter of fact tone that nonetheless couldn't be quite sure of itself.

"No, no, just maybe a freak." Now why did I have to put it so mean against myself? But I was so scared. There I was, still in the doorway, all hope, all dread. Dread that now that Andrea knew this secret thing about me she was going to be really disgusted.

Silence. Silence. More silence. I stood, hands scrunched deep in my pockets, starting to feel like maybe I was a freak after all. Standing waiting like that can do it to you I guess. I thought maybe I should leave. But damned if I would after I'd stuck my neck out like that! I could hardly move anyway, rooted on the threshold, waiting on her.

And she — she was looking at her hands, first the tops, then her palms, not looking up, not looking at me. Two minutes? Three? I couldn't take it anymore! I stood fermenting and then it bubbled over. I had to know one way or another, the best or the worst — whatever! — just so I knew! "Andry?!" A question, almost a demand. She looked up, clutching her one hand in the other, her face flushed.

"Well, uh," she started, paused, then half-laughed, but not a full free laugh, one of those nervous kinds. My heart was hanging in mid-air, straining towards her. There was another moment of the most brimming silence, and she sort of shook her head like she was shaking somehow loose of something and said, "Well for crying out loud Stevie, if you're a freak, then I'm a freak too!" My heart landed with an astonished thud.

I stared at her and she met my look, her eyes big, unblinking, and suddenly I felt I was coming to the surface for the first time in my life, my heart breaking clear up into the fields of those eyes, their teal, the way they took me in. I came a few steps towards her, walking forward in the air that seemed filled with this feeling between us. And it's like that feeling has always been there, but right then it burst wide open — like the sun in the morning when it finally unwraps itself and breaks free of the horizon. It seemed to hang there, bright, turning and turning.

I said, "Jesus, what could be freaky about the way this feels?" Hoping she would know what I meant, that it felt that way to her too. The next thing I knew she was nodding, sliding off the stool and finally, finally! we had our arms around each other! Holding fast and close.

Andrea! Don't ever let me go!

May 5th, 1980 *Tuesday*

How could the world be so much the same and so very different all at once? I don't get it. I walk around and talk in class and eat in the dining hall and wear the clothes I always wear. All exactly like before. But everything is touched, changed, charged, DIFFERENT!

Like our eyes meet when we come down the hall from opposite ends and the whole place lights up somehow! Why can't everybody see it? In class we're sitting there next to each other, nothing new about that, but christ! there's something like an electro-magnetic force field zapping in the half-foot space between us. Zing! And we go to her room and close the door like to talk and nobody looks twice, but we're in there, on the bed, arms wrapped around each other and it's like no kind of talking I have ever done, this new language of half words and the gestures of hands across bodies.

I-Yi! Can't anybody even see it? Well, they better not though, now that I think about it.

May 6th, 1980 *Wednesday*

We hung out with Liddy and Duncan after dinner tonight. First time in how long. I don't know — those two are awfully chummy. I was wondering: you don't suppose? Here I've been thinking how could anybody not notice me and Andry, and maybe all the while this thing under my nose . . . ?

Well, but I guess it is their own business if they do.

Meanwhile, this is like nothing else. Nothing ever has felt like this. I think to myself, oh, so this is what they're talking about, this incredible feels great stuff. I want to write about it, but how do I find the words for this?

May 8th, 1980 *Friday*

Oh god, everything that is happening to me! I mean, here it is Friday, nearly a week since that scene in the art studio, not even a week, and it's like I'm a whole new person. Being with Rik didn't get me ready for this! With her it's like swimming in the ocean — Wheeee! With him it was more like a dead dog paddle in a bathtub.

But how do you write about that ocean? *Do* people write about this stuff? Well, Rita Mae does, we know that. 'Course she's a grown-up, and she makes her own living, and she's not at some goddamn prep school, counting on her dad to send her to college. 'Cause what if someone does find out? Parents are one thing, and bad enough, but what about the other kids? What if Mic knew? Shit, it was that same thing with Rik, always having to hide it. A big bad secret. But this is worse. An affair with a teacher is one thing — scandalous — but this is something else all together, I mean it's QUEER, LEZZY, DYKE stuff!

Oh god, I try not to think about those words. Cause like I said to Andry up in the studio, heading towards her, "What could be freaky about this?" Migod, I just love her! What's so weird about that? It's love! But still, sometimes there'll be this flash thru me when I'm lying next to her, or maybe I'm in class, and she's not even there, and I get this jolt of: No way, people don't do This! Like how could you feel this way, it's gross! Women go with men, not with women! You are twisted! It's not even like I've ever had this thing about growing up and getting married and having babies the way a lot of girls do. But I never thought about this either!

But there's the way it feels! How the fuck am I supposed to argue with that?! How could I ever go back on it, on her, on myself? I don't want to live if I can't feel this way. But maybe I could still feel this way with a boy sometime. Maybe I could.

Maybe I just haven't met the right one yet. I mean, if you think about where I have been — ! Not that Rik was mean or anything, but Christ he could be my father, really he could be, and no wonder I didn't feel the same way for him. I mean, how can you get romantic about your father, for crying out loud. Not to mention your gross uncle! Maybe sometime when I'm in college I'll meet a guy and I'll feel the same way. Just because I feel this way about Andry now doesn't mean I couldn't feel it sometime about some guy, right? Some nice young one! But I know there aren't any guys here I would feel that way about! I been here long enough to know! So I don't have to worry about it right now. And in any case, me and Andry will always be the best of friends, no matter what happens.

May 9th, 1980 *Saturday*

Late afternoon. We're lying stretched out across my bed, just back from jogging together. An hour till dinner and the chair is propped up under the knob of the door.

Am I on top of her? Yes I am. (Did I just write that? Yes I did. Keep on writing too! I got to write or I'm gonna burst with all this! Write about all the ways it doesn't feel freaky!)

With one finger I am tracing the lines of her, along and down her short nose, round the tips of her little ears — god, how I love the way the right one juts out in a small square corner along the top!

— and down to trace the line of her collarbone. IIIII-YI!

So I draw back and rub her nose with mine but in another minute get drawn down again — it just happens! — to nuzzle into her neck; blow, soft! there on her skin.

Then, because, you know what, I just can't take it! I come up for air. Ask her, "How long did you know?"

It takes a second before she comes to, sort of shaking her head, "Know what?"

"You know — how you, uh, felt."

"About you, you mean?" She lifts her head to look up at me, and I scrunch around to hide my face in my pillow with the Matisse cat on it.

"Yeah. About me." My voice coming out muffled.

"Oh god! Ever since I first saw you!" She laughs. I peek out from in the pillow. She's looking out towards the window. I can see the light holding in her eyes.

"*Really?*"

"Yeah. I saw you walking into the dining room, tall, thick braid swaying, long stride, and before I even knew it, I was thinking, 'There's the girl for me!' "

"You did?!" I practically squeal it, squirming just that much further into the pillow.

"Will you come out of there?" she asks, turning. I pause a moment and then turn too, emerging. We're both on our sides now, facing each other. "There," she says, drawing one hand thru my hair. I can feel the loose strands in her fingers. "There. And yes, I did. I thought exactly that." I want to put my hand up to cover over my eyes cause I'm having a shy attack, but I don't. "What about you?" she asks. "How long have you known?" A quick little pang in my body. I want to tell her that of course it happened exactly the same way to me. But that's not true.

"Oh, since hockey anyway," I tell her. Our faces are so close, I can't quite believe it, her eyes steady on mine. I turn a little, look up at the ceiling. "Since that first practice after Christmas when I sat next to you on the bench in the locker room. God! It was like this wind blew up in me, blew me right into you! Close! But I didn't have any words for it then. It just rattled me. D'y'remember? I jumped right up to get my gear!"

Andry nods yes, grin covering one side of her face. She has this sideways grin that is so cute! Her whole mouth slants up to the side. "Well, I had some words for it all right!" she says, "it just took me a while to believe them."

"How come?" I ask, "How come I had to chase you down in the art studio? How come you didn't tell me earlier? You're the one who usually has no problems saying anything!"

She sort of laughs, but it's a laugh on herself. She says, "I was too afraid. Too afraid of what it meant. I was sure you weren't going to be into it."

"Why?" I want to know. She pauses, and at first I don't think she's even going to answer. I can see her considering. "C'mon, c'mon, tell me!" I put a hand on her wrist.

"Well," her words come slow, "I didn't want you to think I was a freak either!" Certainly I understand this! But I see there's still something moving behind her face, something she's keeping back.

"Oh, c'mon! It wasn't obvious that I was — am! — crazy about you?!"

"I wasn't sure!" she slings the words out with passion, and keeps going, "And besides, you were always hanging out with Mr. Wood!" There are more words jumbling up her throat, but I see her set her mouth shut. The top of my head is zinging.

"Yeah," I say quickly, "I guess I was awfully busy getting babysat."

Andry props up on one elbow. "Babysat?" she asks. I nod yeah, but how can I say anything more about it? I can't.

"See, I just didn't know," I say, sliding under her and bringing my hands up to her shoulders, "about *this*." I run my hands down her back, up and down again, over and over. "I didn't know about *this*," I say again, my hands moving the length of her, and then we don't talk anymore until dinnertime.

May 10th, 1980 *Sunday*

I can't do it. Can't write naked.
Not today anyway.

May 11th, 1980 *Monday*

In class Mic talks about "getting at the visceral," and I sit there, stewing. In the last couple of weeks we've been writing these short sketches of people and places and things, a lot of descriptive stuff. Last week I did this description of what it was like in the top of that tall pine tree back home. Of course I left out the part about why I was up there all the time — hiding from my gross disgusting uncle. So when I read it, I feel the part missing. But it's still a pretty good piece I think. Mic liked it too.

But meanwhile! I still feel like I'm going to burst with all this other stuff inside me! It has to go somewhere! The way I feel! It's boiling, boiling, gonna burst! What do I do with it? I should really try harder to write about it in here.

May 13th, 1980 *Wednesday*

I can write this much, the way we were just lying around on my bed this afternoon, laughing, and how we were touching. Touching, touching, touching! And suddenly I remembered that dream from last nite — Kit again, but this time I can see her. She's perched in the very top of a pine, crying. Me — I'm trying to walk towards her, but I'm in this thicket of prickly ash. I keep crawling around the branches, but there's always more and more thicket.

Yak. Lying on the bed with Andrea, I started telling her about the dream, surprised at the way the words kept tumbling out of me. She listened. She really is a good listener. And she knows how I feel about Kit. She does.

God, Kit's been dead since my third form year, but I don't know. The way I still dream about her! Not all the time, but every once in a while, clumps of Kit dreams. God, I wish I could have her right on my chest again, purring thru her sleep. Seems somehow like those were the nights he didn't come, when she was with me.

Of course I didn't tell Andrea about that Philip stuff. But I did tell her about the night I was sort of sleepwalking with Kit, how I got down on the floor with her and how in my sleep I just knew that me and her were out to save the world together, that she understood perfectly that that was our mission, even tho she was a cat. We were making plans together. That's the way it was.

"I want her back!" I said. Jesus. Sounded exactly like a little kid when I said it. Weird. But then the neatest thing, Andrea started singing that little kids' song, the one I really used to like too:

The cat came back the very next day,
Thought she was a goner,
but the cat came back
'cause she wouldn't stay away!

We just started singing it and singing it. God, more than fun! Some kind of perfect moment, up out of all the nights of bad dreams, up out of everything, lying there with our skins touching singing that sweet little song, "the cat came back —"

Something for once all together whole inside.

May 17th, 1980 *Sunday*

How to get at the way the night went, all of it, the bad stuff, the good stuff, the whole story? I guess I've got to begin with the beginning — how we went with Liddy and Duncan to the dance; we've been hanging out with them a lot this last week.

So. We staked ourselves out a corner and started dancing. And I have to say that it looks to me like Duncan and Liddy like dancing together as much as me and Andry do! Course I don't know for sure, but Andry thinks maybe so too.

Anyway, we were there, and they were playing Motown — the fun stuff like "Signed, Sealed, Delivered," and we were dancing all out. Everybody mostly left us alone. I mean, Ken danced in, all by himself, for a few songs, but I didn't mind. He's pretty cool. But then little Jeanie also came in — to dance one with him I think. I wasn't so into that. I don't think Ken was either. Man, does that girl ever remind me of the way I was when I was a third former! Pretty needy, I'd say. She's pushier than I ever was, tho — she started dancing with Ken without asking him if he wanted to dance with her. But after one song it was like she saw something and she hightailed it out of our circle.

Ken kept dancing, and Eliot came in — him and Ken have gotten pretty tight lately. We were making pantomime with all the words, goofing around. It was great! Those boys are both pretty funny. They're not like the other boys. But they left after a bit. To get some punch they said, but I bet it was to get some pot. The DJ started playing this sort of slow one, and Liddy and Duncan went for punch too —

probably really punch — and left us there. So me and Andrea decided to waltz a little. Not that we know how really, but we were dancing arm and arm; sort of close, but not that close either. I mean, you don't TRY to draw attention to yourselves. And it's not like girls don't dance together here. They do sometimes, and it doesn't have to mean anything. Anything at all.

But I looked up, and there, about fifteen feet away, by one of the columns, was Rik, Jeanie standing next to him. He had — there is no other word for it — this LEER on his face. My breath caught in my throat, and Andrea is so quick! She jerked around to see what I was looking at, and even tho Rik was turning away, she caught a flash of it. I heard her hiss under her breath, "That fucking bastard!"

Well. We kept dancing, but it was changed somehow between us, and it was like we both could feel it. I started to sort of lose my shit, I have to say. That leer on his face, like we were dirty somehow, and he knew all about it, every move, every smell, every small sound and the way her hips tremble when I move on her. He could see it all. And I felt like maybe the whole place could see it too, and I started to get this strange panicky feeling. Like in those dreams where you go to school with just your underwear on, and how you feel when suddenly you notice it and see that everybody else has noticed too!

But the weirdest thing was that it got me feeling funny about Andrea, like who is she anyway, maybe she's stranger than I think. I don't feel that way now, and I don't think I ever will again, but I really did feel that way for a while last night. Yuk! It felt terrible! I tried begging off to come back here alone, but Andrea wouldn't let me go myself. She came with me.

By the time we got to my room, I could hardly talk. Andrea was fuming, saying over and over, "That bastard, that bastard! Why can't he just leave you alone?!" I got in bed with all my clothes on, lay there like a lump not talking. She paced. After a while she came over and sat on the edge of the bed. At first I didn't want her to touch me, because of what his look said about all those touches, like we couldn't touch without him and his leer being there too. It made me sick.

But then she stroked my head, sang me some of her songs. I started to feel better, like it made the thoughts of him go away, like it was just her and me again, the way it ought to be. I could talk again. I told her I wanted Rik to leave me alone too. She said he looked like he thought he owned me, and I said — I said it! "Well, he sort of used to!"

"No, no," Andrea was shaking her head back and forth. Hard. "I don't care what you do, you can't ever own anybody. Look at what we do! But it's not like I think I own you!"

How would she ever understand if I didn't tell her the truth? She couldn't! But I needed her to! So I said, "Yeah, but he and me were together longer doing that kind of thing!"

She turned her head toward me, and for a second I saw in her eyes how she had already known that, but had somehow hoped it wasn't true. Now here it was, really true. I had said it. I felt this flash of fear: now I've done it! They'll both hate me now! Rik for my telling, if he ever finds out, Andrea for the fact that I was ever with *him* like that.

But there was only that split second of knowing in her eyes, and then it was like the rest of her had skipped over it. "It doesn't matter how long," she said. "I'll never do that to you! Or look at you that way! Christ! He looked at us like we were two whores! That bastard!"

I lay on my bed, taking in the strokes of her hand, wondering if I could ever feel that kind of indignation in myself. Andry's more that way than me — fiery. Rik was right when he said she's sort of like a James Dean! But to tell the truth, I felt a little defensive on his account. So OK, he was a jerk at the dance, but he's not all bad either. I think if he really knew the way it made me feel, he wouldn't look at us that way.

But I wasn't going to tell Andrea that! And since I was feeling better, it was a moot point. We got up after a while, took showers, and made this plan — for the first time! — to meet up in my room after check-in so we could sleep the night together. I didn't want to say good night to her. Not at all. I knew I didn't feel like fooling around, but I didn't want her to go away either.

Around twelve, my door swung open, fast, and she slipped in, even faster. She was grinning that sideways grin, a little shy. I was shy too. Something about the way we had decided to spend a night — a whole night! — together gave this serious weight to things. We got in bed, and we were talking, sort of kissing, and Andrea reached to shut the light, and everything was suddenly swallowed up in the darkness. The kind of darkness that can eat you alive. But wasn't that her voice in my ear? Yes, but in the dark, it was still like she could be anybody, and oh christ, but I got feeling really really weird! Different than before, a kind of reeling inside, around and around like I was in a huge sink, circling and about to be sucked down the drain. Andrea was touching me, but I wasn't moving. She said, "Stevie?"

I didn't answer at first. That was her voice, right? But I needed to see her! "Can we leave the light on?" I asked. She paused in the dark next to me, some consideration, I don't know what, moving thru her, and I said, nearly pleading, "Please?" She reached back up and clicked the lamp on again. After the dark, the light spilling out was suddenly harsh, but what a relief! This was really Andry next to me! Andrea Snyder and nobody else.

"Are you OK?" She leaned over me.

"I just get nervous sometimes in the dark," I told her. "Do you mind if we leave it on?" I could tell she wasn't crazy about the idea, and I felt like such a baby! But I wasn't going to be able to take that sucked up feeling. How would I ever explain it? I don't understand it myself! I said again, "Do you mind?"

"It's OK with me," she said, and I got the sense that she had decided it just had to be. We talked some more, about the summer, and how she's going to be on this paint crew back in Northampton with some of her friends. She said they are really fun, and maybe I could be on the crew too. As it stands, the only plan I have now is to go back to Georgeville. So maybe I could. If I dare bring it up to the folks that is. Dad will probably think I should either stay in Vermont or work for him, yak. And truth to tell, I may have pushed him enough for the year!

But anyway, we were talking, things easing after that bit of weirdness on my part, and then, from far away, I was hearing Andrea say, "Are you falling asleep Stevie?" I was!

She let me go. I slept, dreaming my way all thru that first night with her. Dreams interwoven with these spots of waking to her arms around me. Another time she was lying on her back, and I wrapped my arms around her, and still in her sleep, she turned and nuzzled into me! The sweetest thing!

That was not all tho.

If you can do it, you can write it, right?

Well . . . . . . to begin with, I woke up first, just like I did over break, every morning. But this time I wasn't embarrassed to prop myself up on one elbow and look and look, trying to take all of her in. Very sweet! Lying curled towards me, one arm tucked over the top of the blanket, the other arched up over the pillow, her face gone slack and soft, cheeks slightly moving with her breath in and out. And I remembered how I stared at her same sleeping body back in Northampton, wondering — like Joni Mitchell singing in that Rainy Night House — "who in the world you might be."

But even as I was lying there, I stopped thinking anything. Because all of a sudden it was as if all I could do was feel her, some essence of her, some "her-ness" rising up from her, not ghostly, more the way a bowl of hot soup gives off a part of itself in the steam that rises up out of it. Not that I would even see anything, but there it was anyway. Her. HER.

And that's when she woke up, her eyes blinking, and then, turning up to meet mine, the smile that opened her face, the way she brought her arms up around me, her body all warm with sleep, bringing me off my elbow back down to the blankets, back down to press against her in that warmth, the sheet twisting all around us.

Well. We were just lying like that for a while, sort of pressing against each other and I was stroking her. But then this funny stuff happened. I don't know what else to call it. It's happened before too. This time, I don't know, I had sort of climbed on top of her, and we both were moving whatever way it felt right, but then this feeling like queasiness but it wasn't in my stomach, started to spread in me, first in my legs, and then in my arms. I tried to pretend it wasn't there, but that didn't work. Then I told it to go away, but it was just bubbling up like the build-up to a scary scene in a movie when the music starts getting weird and you know something bad is going to happen. And the bad wasn't Andrea, it was something about ME. Cause when I closed my eyes, I felt myself something huge and ominous hanging over her, and then it wasn't even me I saw, but them. I was one of them. I pushed off with one arm and rolled off her, back up against the wall.

"What?" she said, "What?" Her hands reaching for my face. I didn't want to tell her of course. I pulled the end of the sheet over my head.

"What did I do wrong? What did I do?"

Me shaking my sheeted head, voice coming out

136

muffled, "It's not you, it's never you, never — ever — never — you."

I could hear the edge of irritation rising in her voice, "Well, I don't see who else it could be Stevie, I don't see anybody else here in this room except you and me. I mean, if you like somebody else or something, or I don't know, if you just don't like me, I mean, tell me!" Her voice rising to a small but almost desperate pitch that raked a sharp gash in my chest.

"Oh god, Andry, no, I love you! I really do! It's just . . ."

Long pause. I burrowed down deeper under the blankets like a small animal.

"It's just WHAT?"

"It's these, well, monsters, bad guy things that eat children and little cats, boogie men or just men, I don't know. It's like the way I won't go into a dark room with any guy because you never know, maybe they'll kind of pin you to the couch and get on top of you. So when *I* get on top of *you* like that, I feel like I'm turning into one of them! Monstrous. Like I'm making you do it or something. Like I'm going to eat you up."

The blankets were moving now in waves, little earthquakes all around, and then peering at me in the dim, moist under-blanket world was the pointed face of Andrea. "Stevie," she was saying, "Stevie, I love it! I love the way you touch me and how it feels. I wouldn't let you do it if I didn't!"

"You sure?"

Her face quizzical, like I was some puzzle she had never thought of. "Of course I am. Why wouldn't I be?"

I couldn't say. Her hand moving lightly across my cheek.

"Monsters have great terrible hairs sprouting from their chins, don't they?" she said, "This chin feels pretty smooth to me, dearie." She swung an arm up and the blankets lifted, red folds spilling down onto the floor. "You don't look like a monster either! You're way too scrawny. And besides, your eyes are kind."

She had pulled herself up now and was straddling my hips, rising over me. She sat there a moment, hands on her own hips, looking down into my face. What she saw, I'm not sure, but her voice softened. "Do I look like a monster to you?"

The thing was that for a moment she did seem that way — well, it wasn't her exactly, it was some shadow between her and me, some cloudy mass bulking up like a thunderhead gathering storm. Maybe that's what she saw, its shadow streaking across my face.

"Stevie!" Her whisper calling me. "Stevie! Look at me! *Me.*" I did. I looked at her. The cloud breaking up, wisps drifting off, and it was that sense of her again I got, that essence of her like buckets of sap boiled down to a warm jar of maple syrup and all you need is a whiff to know it's the real thing. Andrea Snyder looked at me, and I looked back.

That's when she brought her face to mine. "Can I touch you?" she asked. "Do you want me to?" And I did! This sudden welling up inside me, overripe peach splitting open. I nodded. I told her yes. Then she was moving her hands all up and down me, and at first I was wondering when she was going to make her move. But she didn't, it wasn't like that at all, she just kept stroking the length of me, all up and down my arms both of them, and then my right leg, along and up the bump of my hip. Somewhere in there I stopped thinking, I was just something feeling her touch, just somebody feeling myself starting to move with her, some piece way down inside me rising up towards her fingers across my skin, my voice saying her name, and reaching for her face and needing her mouth on mine. And her rolling off my body, but leaning down closer over me, propped up on one elbow, kissing me, one hand still moving everywhere, then riding down the little round of my belly, and me arching up to meet her palm, the two of us back and forth, her bending down and me rising up like dancing lying there on the bed, filling the room with our motion, dancing, dancing, our bodies streaming out in colors.

And I was drinking her in, letting her fill me as she went deeper and deeper, and then I was riding the ocean inside me, the swells rising, my body riding up on a wave, a great wave that was lifting me and lifting me and then it paused, and I was floating on its white crest, and then another surge higher, and another pause, and I hung there weightless under some vast expanse of sky and finally up up up, the final surging launching me up into the face of the sky itself, my whole body opening up to it like a freeze-frame of a flower in release, its petals exploding out in great bursts, and then down, down, soft, back in bed next to her, and then laughing with the sheer relish of it, and Andrea kissing me, her eyes liquid delight.

May 18th, 1980 *Monday*

ONLY THREE WEEKS MORE UNTIL
G-R-A-D-U-A-T-I-O-N!
The countdown begins here. Only 21 more days!!!!!!!!

What else is there to say after that last entry? I still can't believe I wrote all that down! God, if I'm going to be writing stuff like that, I better make absolutely sure that nobody ever sees this journal.

Maybe I am just too suspicious, but this funny thing happened with Liddy at lunch. I don't know for sure, but it scared the shit out of me. I don't know.

Well, but, there I was sitting alone. The dining hall is not my favorite place these days; I like to eat and get out of there. But she came over. At first that was kind of nice; we were talking about the hop and how much fun it was to dance all together like that. But then she asked why me and Andrea took off so fast.

Well. I made up some stupid lie about getting tired of the scene, thinking that would be the end of it. But she sat there, rolling up those pasty strands of spaghetti. I could see that she was turning something over in her mind. My insides gripped: "uh-oh!"

"Huh," she said, "I thought maybe you'd gotten

sick. You didn't look so good. I mean, we were standing kind of far off, but it looked to me like you'd seen a ghost or something, just stopping like that! Betz thought mebby Andrea had punched you in the stomach!"

I'm sure I grimaced. "Not exactly," I said. And then I didn't know what else to say. I'm such a bad liar! Give me paper, a pen and some time, and I can make up all kinds of stories. But not on the spot! So I fumbled. Said something about how actually I had suddenly thought my tampon was leaking. Shit. Must have been desperate to come up with that excuse!

But that Liddy! She doesn't let things go easy! She kinda went huh, and paused, forking the pasta into her mouth. I watched her chewing it over. Then I looked down. Maybe a little too fast. "Huh," she said, "That's funny. It really looked to me like you saw something you didn't like." The end of her sentence going up the slightest touch in that questioning tone.

"It was the idea of bleeding all over the place that I didn't like!" I said. Some clumsy humor there Stevie! Shit tho, I thought maybe she was going to keep pressing me. Thank god she didn't. But I saw this moment on her face, this look like she didn't quite believe me.

Damn, I wonder how much she saw. I wonder if she'll say anything to Andrea about it. And what would Andry say? She's so uncrazy about Rik, she might slip up. Or worse? Christ, it makes me so nervous just thinking about it!

Well. I took off pretty quick after that. Maybe it was kind of rude, but that look on her face! A certain sharpness, like somehow she knew there was more than I was telling her. I think maybe she would love to pry it out of me. Or maybe out of Andrea? Oh, please keep your mouth shut Andry! Please, please, please! He'll kill me if word ever gets out. I know he'll just KILL me.

May 19th, 1980 *Tuesday*   20 MORE DAYS

SHITFUCKDAMN

Why do I even fucking care what I got on that miserable AP? Why do I even give a shit!!!!!!

All right, all right, a 4 isn't that bad, now is it? No, it's not that bad, but it's not good enough either, damitall!! 'Specially because I *know* I'm smarter than some of those kids who got fives. 'Specially Eliot.

Shit why can't I feel today the way I felt when I was taking the test? I really didn't care then; what I'd just written was the point, not the goddamn grade.

I bet you some high and mighty straitlaced asshole was the one who graded my essay, somebody who thinks Shakespeare is the ruler of all. That's why I got a 4 and not a 5. Now if someone like Mic had been the reader...

May 20th, 1980 *Wednesday*   19 MORE DAYS

I wasn't there, but I can see it all right! The

sharp slight Andry moving back and forth in that shallow alcove that passes for a gallery around here, setting her stuff for the Senior Art Show. She's fussing, shifting her sculptures from one spot to another, never looking up, solely intent. That's how she gets. He, meanwhile, is walking down the hall, one hand in his pocket. And he's almost upon her before she notices him, but when she does, she sort of jumps — tho not hardly so you'd notice.

She told me tonite, after dinner, after coffee, Cokes and butts. I had noticed she was a little off or something, but didn't know why. So she started telling me. At first I was kind of saying, well, what do you expect? Because after all, Andrea's sculptures are of women. NAKED women. I sort of think she's got to be ready to take some grief for that. 'Cause this ain't the Guggenheim here. Of course some of the guys are going to make faces.

"It wasn't just faces, Stevie!" When she burst out with that, I kind of backed off. I didn't know she was going to be so touchy about this stuff. But you never know. And even tho I backed off, she kept going on about it anyway — told me again about how Rik did sort of have a look, tho not as blatant as the one Saturday nite.

"So what was it then?" Stupid nosey me, asking questions when the answers aren't going to be anything I want to hear. Damn.

So. That's when Andrea told me about how he *touched* the statues, ran his fingers up the legs — YI! And the comment he made. Christ. Something about how much hands-on research Andrea must have done to make her statues so life-like.

But maybe he didn't mean it that way! Andrea

says she knows that's exactly what he meant, but I think maybe he meant that she's got a good eye or something —

— or maybe he's just jealous now. That kind of makes sense, doesn't it? I can understand that. God, I never thought he would get bothered enough to get jealous, but maybe it did get to him a little, seeing us dance, and that's why he slipped up like that. I can see why Andrea would be ticked, but I don't think he meant it that mean. I do know him a little! It was a slip. He's not that bad. I wish she didn't have to go get so pissed about it.

May 21st, 1980 *Thursday*   18 MORE DAYS

Ow ow ow ow ow ow ow ow ow ow ow!

The ironic thing is that Mom actually called me tonight. Course that's remarkable enough in itself. But the irony is that she called to tell me that she and Dad talked over this idea of me on the paint crew, and they both think it's a good idea.

Shit. Just when it's too late. Andrea's not going to want me in Northampton this summer. She's not going to want me ever again, period. Shit, shit, shit!

I was with her a bit tonight tho — with Duncan and Liddy, in the coffee room. Ken and Eliot came over to our table — they have been so chummy with the four of us lately. They wanted to know if we would help out with the Senior Prank Saturday night. The plan is to get Phillip's Volvo into the dining hall — a charming conversation piece for Sunday brunch.

We all said yes. Even me! But what the hell. At least I can show Andrea that I'm not the teacher lover she thinks I am.

I bet you it's too late tho. She took off around eight. Hardly would look at me as she turned away. I was watching her going tho, and when I looked up, I saw Liddy watching me.

But I can't worry about that. Oh god, it's Andrea, Andrea, Andrea! Aggggggggg. I want to come home!! Please take me back!

Oh god, it's too late. Too late for being with her, too late for me all together. I feel like a small dead thing in the road, run over and wasted. Least I could do is get a poem out of it. But I know it's too late for that too.

May 24th, 1980 *Sunday*   15 MORE DAYS

JESUS WHAT SHE DID!!!!!!!!!!!!

Bellows called a special meeting of the Seniors tonite. That was so he could berate us for the "vicious vandalism" and the "shameless attack on a teacher's integrity." He said there will be no Senior Dance unless the "individuals involved" come forward.

Oh Christ, I know that if anybody saw my face they'd be on to me. So I wore my baseball cap.

A little cap ain't going to save me from Rik tho. I think I have really had it now. I know he must want to kill me. I mean, KILL me.

God, why did I let her go off like that? Why

didn't I stop her? But I was busy with Eliot and Ken in our little offshoot of a Senior prank, gluing the classroom doors shut. I don't know why I went along with that. But they had told me it wouldn't be such a big deal, that it wouldn't cause any permanent damage. Which, evidently, is far from the truth. I wish I had stuck with the car prank. But about twenty kids were already there when we arrived, including Duncan and Liddy; they didn't need our help. And Ken and Eliot said they did.

Jesus, what an idiot I was.

So. There we were, the four of us, kneeling and swabbing that sticky stuff up and down the sides of the doors, when Andrea all of a sudden straightened and headed down the hall, saying she'd be right back. I looked up, asked towards her back where she was going, and she said over her shoulder that she had her own little trick to pull, pay no never mind, she'd be back soon enough. Well, it bugged me that she left, that always bugs me, no matter what, but I didn't really think of it beyond that. So me and Ken and Eliot kept on, smearing glue, and it was sort of fun for a while there, I have to admit. Scary too, like in a suspense movie, because what if the night watchman came, but Ken said he wouldn't be making his rounds up thru the classroom halls until at least 3:30.

After a while, it occurred to me to wonder where Andrea had gone, and I got this first inkling, like an "uh-oh!" without knowing exactly what about. Somehow tho I knew to run right down the hall for Rik's classroom.

Sure enough! There she was, all the way in the rear of the room, facing the back wall, looking like she was writing at the chalkboard, but it was on the cinder block wall instead. A certain horror seized me whole, like shaved ice dumped into my blood.

"What are you doing!" The croak out of me. The room was pretty dark, but in the glow from the parking lot lights outside I started to see something I couldn't believe, even tho I was seeing it, this writing on the walls — lipstick scrawled words I couldn't yet make out. Andrea swung around to look at me, and as I walked towards her, I saw her face, a look I've never seen, proud and furious and pleading all at once.

She turned back to the wall, whispering loudly back to me, on and on, stuff I never thought I'd hear her say, stuff, stuff!!!! About how Rik was a bastard who had it coming to him, how he thinks he can fuck around with students and get away with it, how he was an asshole for making that comment about her "hands on research." On and on. On and on. I stood frozen in the wash of her words.

But then I broke, ran up behind her, grabbing her hand. Started reading, "Rik Wood preys on students! Rik Wood is a lecher!!!" Over and over, ringing the room everywhere in a large dark scrawl of red. I think I made this crying noise, I don't know, it was like I was swamped under this very big bad wave. Of what I don't know, but swept under. Drowning.

'Cause it wasn't just him, it was me too. It was me too! Why does Andrea have to scream it to the whole world! Everybody in school knows I used to hang out with him, who else could it mean but me! How could she do this to me!!!!

HOW COULD SHE!!!!!!!

147

But oh christ, don't lose your shit here. Remember, there's a story to be told. Now c'mon!

Oh, but fuck the story! That's enough of the story to make the point!!!!!!!!!!!

But no, Stevie, don't leave out the next part, the part where you were gripping her hand so hard that this flash of amazed pain cut across her face, the part where she dropped the lipstick and the thing clattered to the floor. 'Specially don't forget the part when something in you snapped all together and you sprang for the door, running all the way back to the dorm. Coming back here alone.

Alone.

Who doesn't deserve who around here?

But no matter, I've had it now. Really had it.

*May 25th, 1980 *Monday*   14 MORE DAYS*

FROGS IN THE RAIN

Nights when the wet road glistens
   like a black mirror
and the headlights make bright white rivers,
they are there, perched
like stone still statues of themselves
on the dark sheen of tar,
contemplating the sound a drop makes
when finally it strikes something solid.

Great washes of car light
bearing down on their unblinking meditations,
they are little buddhas, squatting transfixed,

148

and for miles the road is splattered,
little wet piles where they have gone down under
    tires,
knowing in one instant the sound their lives
    make
when something solid finally strikes.

*May 26th, 1980 *Tuesday**   13 MORE DAYS

I haven't seen Rik at all! He must be lying low, that's it. Maybe he's going to come for me later. I don't know. I don't know. But one good thing is that at least Bellows is making it really clear that the stuff on the wall is just "vicious rumor mongering." I don't think he's even questioning Rik at all. So maybe Rik isn't so mad. I mean, he's not really in trouble or anything, right?

But Bellows meanwhile really has it in for the graffiti artist! God, I'm glad it wasn't me! 'Cause is he ever ripped. He hauled me into his office today and I've never seen anything get to him quite like this; he had that feel to him like someone had insulted his mother. Insulted her really bad. I sat there, bottled up in a fit of nervousness in the chair.

"I have been led to believe, Stephanie," he said, pulling at one sleeve, "that you might think yourself justified in such a stunt."

His trick almost worked. I almost shot back, "Who told you that!" But I sat on myself and said, "I don't know what you are talking about. Mr. Wood and I have always been friends. I don't treat my friends that way."

Bellows sat there, nodding, looking off to the wall, a nod that said uh-huh, sure, right. He asked me really icy-like if I might be able to make any guesses, then, about who might be responsible. I shook my head no. I didn't say a word more than I had to. I stuck to my innocence. I know he can't prove anything.

But still I can't believe the fucking trouble she got me into!!!!!! Some friend.

It's a damn good thing she's been leaving me alone. I may have to see her in class and at ball, but that doesn't mean I have to talk to her.

I don't even have to write about her!

May 27th, 1980 *Wednesday*   12 MORE DAYS

It was my fault for giving Mic that damn frog poem. What the fuck was I thinking? I might have just as well written an actual confession! Way to go, Stevie.

She called me up after class. I shambled up to her desk, not wanting to look her in the face. Once everybody else was gone, she got up and shut the door. Which made me want to run out of there so bad. She came and sat back down behind her desk. I stood at the other side. I just couldn't look. When I tried, she was looking right into me, those eyes locking me in. I had to turn my head. "That was some poem you wrote there, Stevie," she said. I couldn't answer her. "You want to talk about it?" I shook my head and the next thing I knew I was forcing out a stupid lie about how I had to go meet Williams to talk about my final paper.

God, I'm lying all over the place these days. I'm still a really shitty liar tho.

But she let me go anyway. And I practically bolted out of there. I just can't tell her. I know she must think I am a slut. And a thug. And now a liar too. There's nothing to explain.

There's nothing to explain to anybody. Because I don't know how to explain it to myself. I can't even kid myself anymore that it was love — I know the difference now! So why did I do that stuff with him? God, I don't want to talk to anybody about it. I mean, look at Andrea — I know she thinks it's so gross that I ever slept with him.

Shit! I get so scared that I am going to come thru some door and walk right into him. God if he gets me in a corner he's going to kill me right then and there. Walking around school I've got that paranoid all the time feeling again — just like I did after vacation.

Please, just let me out of here!!!

May 28th, 1980 *Thursday*   11 MORE DAYS

Why do I have to wait eleven goddamn days to get out of this place! Shit I wish I had a car. I would be gone so fast. I don't even care where I go, just away, away, away.

The whole fucking school knew before me. They were probably talking about it at the next table, and there I was, sitting alone by the window. Too bad I got to eat. If I just got more allowance, I'd go to the snack bar, I wouldn't even set foot in that friggin dining hall, it's too much like flying down into a pond ringed round with rifles. Like duh, duh, duh! Fly on!

But there I was, trying to eat fast and get the hell out when Liddy came over and sat with me. When she's with Duncan, she's not so bad somehow. But tonite she was getting nosy again. God! It scares me to death! Like the way she was the other day too, asking me about why I stopped dancing. But god, if I thought I was antsy before! This time she had the pleasure — I'm sure it was! — of being the first to inform me of how Andrea went to Bellows today and confessed — not only to the graffiti, but to the glue job too! I can't believe it! I couldn't even keep chewing. Damn hard to hide the roiling up in me; I took a hit of my juice. And all the while Liddy was really watching me — to see how I would react I'm sure. Jesus.

So then she told me how she talked to Andrea herself, up in the studio this afternoon — pang! goes my stupid heart! I can see her up there — damn, look, she fucked you over, and this doesn't make up for it, OK! And how Andrea said that she had a "personality conflict" with Rik, and that she had lost her head and wrote on the wall the worst possible thing she could think of.

Liddy wanted to know what I thought about that, this "personality conflict" bit. Oh Christ, I didn't want to talk about it! Why doesn't she leave me

alone? I just said how I thought Andrea was right —
that that was just about the worst thing you could
say about a teacher.

Well. That's when Liddy said this funny thing,
about how if it had been her up there doing the
writing, she wouldn't have left it at that — because
she can think of worse things to say about Rik
Wood. Plenty more and all true too, she said. I
didn't say anything! I couldn't! I just shrugged. So
what does that mean Andrea told her?! What if my
dear X-friend told her what I told my dear X-friend?
And then got Liddy to see it from her point of
view?! I almost thought I saw that in Liddy's look.
God if she knows, I'm dead for sure, she's not the
kind to keep her mouth shut. It will be all over
school. And if Rik doesn't plan on finishing me off
already, he for sure will then.

I can't think about it now.

Just damn that Andrea! Maybe she thinks
she's doing this very noble thing, getting me off the
hook with the gluing stunt. But still — the other
damage is done! I mean, it's a good thing that
Bellows is defending Rik, because probably that will
keep him from killing me, but meanwhile, I know
the whole school is thinking about it. And no matter
what Bellows is saying, I know some people are
wondering if it is true, and I know how your mind
runs when it comes to that kind of shit. Like you
start imagining what somebody looks like in bed
with all her clothes off and somebody on top of her!
Why doesn't Andrea just make a movie of it and
show it to the whole school! And let's not forget the

trustees and while you're at it, all the parents and the alumni and all their families and friends! Let them all see it! See me!

But what a martyr Andrea gets to be now! I guess Bellows came down hard on her, let her have it with both barrels on the lecture end of things. I bet you she got the full blast of that fury I saw in him the other day just looking for someplace to storm. Plus she has to spend this last week painting. Like the gym. This is Senior week! When all the little underclassmen are struggling with final exams, but we seniors get to kick back, take it easy at our country club of a prep school. And of course now the Senior Dance is on again, and Andrea is the only one who can't go. Not that she probably gives a flying.

But even if she did, she deserves it! Well, maybe not the lecture she got! The rest tho! Not for the reasons Bellows thinks, but yeah, she deserves it all right! And she better not be thinking I'm going to forgive her! Even if she did take the whole rap!

*May 30th, 1980 *Saturday**   9 MORE DAYS

Oh god what I just saw! At the dance — him, really him, like for the first time. I can't even write it yet. But I will. Even if I have to do it sideways. That fucker. That miserable fucker.

It makes me want to go tell Andrea. It really does. But she'd just say "I told you so!" So I won't. And that is that. Period.

Well, I wrote a last assignment for Mic after all. Just went over to Adams and gave it to her. So much for the frog life.

But shit, Mic looked so harassed; end of semester is always a wicked crunch time for teachers, worse than it is for students.

But still — I know, after everything she's ever said, she'll make a little time for me. 'Specially after she reads my story.

I hope she likes it. *I* like it. Even if it does make me miss Andrea. Like crazy.

Little Hay Girl and the Color Cat
A Grim-No-Longer Tale

Once upon a time there was a little girl who lived by herself in the vast airy loft of a barn. She had been there so long that she could barely remember the first day she had been brought there, how a big bearded farmer had taken her by the hand and led her up up up into the mounds of hay. Indeed, she had been there so long that she could not really remember the world she had come from.

All day in the barn sunlit breezes blew in and out and swallows flitted above the girl's head in the rafters. Sometimes in the morning she would climb up to the big hay doors and sit on the broad sill, looking out as the birds swooped in great plunges and loops, skimming the tossing tops of long grasses.

Then in the afternoon, after their morning of hunting and napping, the barn cats came to be with her. The girl spent long hours playing hide and seek and tag with them. Sometimes they would sit together in a circle and the cats would tell her rambling tales of their adventures, stories of how blue the pond looked in the morning light, what falling rain felt like on their whiskers, the feel of dew under their paws. From their stories, the girl thought the world must be a wonderful place indeed.

Then as the darkness seeped in around them, one by one the cats slipped off into the night that was turning scarlet into purple into darkest blue. The girl would watch as the last thin tail bobbed down the hay and would sit down to her supper of berries and grain and milk. Every day the cats brought her what things they could.

After supper she would swing on the old rope that hung from the ceiling, long arching flights over the hay, up into the eaves and back again, lifting her feet so the deepening shadows could not grab her by the ankles and drag her down. In air she would dream of the world, of the pond and fields, of mountains and the feel of rain on her face. Finally, too tired for more, she would lie herself reluctantly down in her straw bed.

And then, lying there, a small girl alone in the dark, she would pray that the beast would not come, pray that it would leave her be. And on some nights it did not come. But on others, how many she could not tell, it did, the strange long-tailed beast on two legs that brought its huge weight down, lapping at her with a heavy scaled tongue until her whole body was in terrible fire, burning her alive. This would go on and on endlessly until suddenly the beast would be gone. And then the dark would turn and turn till morning came finally clambering over night's broken back to return day to the world. And every morning she was still alive.

And so it went and she wore long clothes that covered her and never spoke of it. But time passed, and the girl was growing, her legs and arms longer; she looked less and less like a girl, her features and form beginning to take their womanly shape.

One day a new cat appeared in the barn. No one could say where she had come from. She was the most beautiful cat the girl had ever seen, with crystal green eyes and a fluffy coat of every color, so bright that bits of color glimmered up as she moved. The girl could not take her eyes from the new cat. They played, pairing up in the afternoon games. Gradually the girl came to love the color cat as she had never loved anything else. Every morning she thanked the stars blinking out above her that she had lived thru another night and could see her new friend again.

One rainy afternoon the color cat called the hay girl over to the furthest corner of the loft. One drop of rain after another dripped into the hay next to them. The cat reached out her left paw and with her paws sheathed, slipped the girl's sleeve up her arm. There, revealed, was the burnt skin. The girl flushed a bloody red and dropped down, hiding her face in her hands. And now the drips fell on the top of her head, and still she could not look up, the silence between each tiny splash a space blazing with every night the beast had ever come, firing her. A small splash and then the flames and a splash again, and the drumming of rain on the tin roof rapping louder and louder until the girl looked up and a drop fell to her face like a kiss. When she sat up, moving slowly, it ran down her cheek.

The color cat was still there, watching, her eyes full of light, one single bright round tear caught in her whiskers. She scooped it with a folded paw and held it out, a brilliant clear stone the girl took in her own hand.

"Hang this about your neck," said the cat, "it will help you where you have never had help before and needed it." Then the color cat was gone.

By this time it was already late in the day, and the girl took a piece of twine and tied the stone around her neck, then sat down to her supper. Then she lay down and slept deeply, dreaming. She dreamt she was a fish swimming her joyous way out to sea and

woke to the sound of the beast, tail shuffling in the hay, coming towards her. The girl sat up, clutching the stone at her throat.

"Who are you?" she cried.

The creature paused, grunting.

"Who are you?" the girl cried again.

"It is of no consequence to you, Hay Girl," the beast replied, his huge shape looming over her, down, down, and then he was full over her. But then out of that very darkness falling came glinting splinters of light, dancing flashings and the girl remembered the words of the color cat.

"Help," said the girl to herself, "Help. Help when I need it. Help!" She yanked the stone up from around her neck, and held it high, its clarity suddenly blazing like a torch in the vast recesses of the old loft. In that light she could see the cats crouching, their eyes yellow, their tails swishing back and forth.

"Help!" hissed the cats, "help when you need it!"

Then the girl looked up in the face of the beast, and the shadows fell from him, peeled away like scales from a snake, falling to the floor like bits of ash.

It was the farmer whose face she saw, the man who had brought her to this place. His features twisted in the unrelenting scrutiny of the light. He turned away when her eyes met his.

"Get off me!" cried the Hay Girl, and when there was no movement in that mountain of flesh, she thrust her arms and legs, her body and everything in her up, up, up.

And off he did go, rolling down the hay mound, a heavy tumbling and crash as he fell down the chute to the floor far below.

The girl jumped to her feet. The cats were all about her now, prancing, exulting. Up thru them came the color cat, one paw outstretched.

"Congratulations, my friend, you have prevailed," she said. The girl swooped the cat up into her arms and felt her throaty purr against her chest. And then they all celebrated, dancing and playing far into the night until the girl fell into her bed, asleep instantly.

She slept soundly and woke to the long thin rays of dawn shooting thru the cracks in the hayloft doors. Her ears had caught the softest meow and she turned to see the color cat coming towards her. Suddenly she knew the cat had come to tell her it was time to leave this place.

She propped herself up on stiffened arms, saying, "But you must come with me, color cat!"

And the cat pulled up to where she was, pausing. "I do not know if you are ready to have me with you, my friend," she said.

And she was right, for suddenly the girl was afraid to bring the cat into her arms, even tho they had danced so freely the night before and, surrounded by the other cats, the girl had held her tightly to her chest. She started crying, burying her head in the straw, and could not stop until she looked up and saw the color cat again. It was then too that she saw the light of the day coming full upon them both. She called the cat to her.

The color cat drew towards the girl slowly, carefully, but when she was almost upon her, she stopped, waiting. The girl said, "Please. Come." And then, paw by paw, the cat brought her body onto the girl's chest. And even tho the girl's fear was ferocious within her, something new was taking hold, and it was this the girl felt in her hands as she ran them the length of the cat. The cat bent her head, licking each tear that had spilled onto the girl's face. Then the cat's rough tongue was full on her chest, licking her, spreading a glorious new warmth thru her body. The girl began to laugh, and then she was licking back and with each lap against the cat's chest the fur fell away until the girl saw before her another young woman, dark dark hair and the same clear eyes that had gazed on her from the face of the cat. Seeing her, she knew the farmer's curse was entirely broken.

"Shall we go?" the woman who had once been a cat asked her. The hay girl — now no longer a girl, but a woman herself, nodded. Together they walked to the rope, each grasping the large knot firmly, one foot and then the other, and then they were in the air, the whole world finally before them.

June 2nd, 1980 *Tuesday* 6 MORE DAYS

Three days later, now maybe I can finally write about this. Outright, I mean. My froggishness notwithstanding, I have been knocking myself out for months to really say shit in here, how things really happened, like how things went down with Andrea, what we were really doing and how it felt. But here's this thing I have barely written about! Like some hole in my life, a black hole in space, swallowing all the words. Swallowing them whole.

But no, no, NO!!!!! I SAW this. That stupid old joke about carpenters never believing anything until they saw it, that's me. Fuck, and here I thought I had stepped clear out from that wall. But oh no, the wall lives on still! Well, but not altogether either. Maybe I'm doing just what I said I could do, seeing a bit and then later a bit more.

Saturday night, there I was, wandering around campus like a lost shadow under the trees. And there *it* was — the Senior Dance, that big canopy tent, yellow light spilling out, the music floating towards me. I moved towards it, slipped in, not looking so much at any one person as I was looking over them all. Kind of positioning myself in the far end, back behind some empty chairs, half leaning up against one of the poles. It was like watching from some other planet. That's really what it felt like, seeing all those kids dancing out there on that grassy dance floor, the girls in the boys' arms. Laughing and smiling, whirling around in circles together. From far, far away, I was watching it all.

How do I finally just write this? The actual thing itself, out beyond all the dragons and captains, farmers and cats?

By just writing it! Yes. This is what I saw: Rik standing over at the other end of the floor, a cup in his hand. I saw him, I don't think he saw me. And standing right next to him was little Jeanie. Right next to him. He was laughing about something, I couldn't tell what. She was laughing too. Then the song that had been playing ended and another one started up, a sort of slow one. I saw Rik turn, oh so graciously! to Jeanie, reaching for her hand with his free one. I could practically see her blushing from where I stood. Rik tossed his cup in a garbage can and led her out onto the floor. And he didn't dance her close, but you know what? He didn't have to. I watched them, watched from back in the shadows where he couldn't see me. He was talking to her, bending over so his words could reach her ears. She was laughing, and all the while he was holding her at that respectable length apart. But I knew! I knew by the way she simpered along with him, I could see

it in the curve of his neck as he bent to speak to
her. He's already taken her to bed! I know him! I
can see it!

And standing there I suddenly saw that he
thinks he's untouchable. A hundred Andreas could
scrawl on a hundred walls, and it will still be fine
for him to waltz young women out on the dance
floor, waltz them right into bed. Isn't that nice for
him? No wonder I never wanted to see it!

But I did. Saturday nite. And I looked away,
looked at my sneakers for a while, because I couldn't
fucking stop all this everloving seeing! And then I
scanned the floor again. Saw so many kids dancing
with kids! And I started thinking about how I have
never done that my whole time here, how that
Motown hop with A. and L. and D. was the first
time in my whole Bristol career! And why was that?!
Because Rik took all my time, because I could never
get close to anybody on account of that big heavy
secret! That fall day fourth form year when I saw
my class coming together with all the new kids, I
should have gotten right up from where I was
sitting with Rik and gone and sat with them.

I have missed so much here! And it's gone
forever! And where was I? In his goddamn bed! It
wasn't a good trade off at all. Not worth it. But I
didn't want to know that then.

I do remember telling him I wouldn't have done
it for anybody else. I was fourteen and that's what I
told him. It was true. I remember that once I was
thirteen I decided that if Philip ever tried anything
on me again, I would slug him! He was already a

few years gone by then, but he was supposed to come and visit. He didn't end up coming, thank god, but I remember that's why I was thinking about it.

But then, one year later, here was this handsome teacher who was really smart and who paid lots of attention to me! A lot more than Granite ever did! And he told me he loved me! So I figured it couldn't be the same thing as Philip. And that's why I did what he wanted. Plus I needed somebody so bad, that's why I did what he wanted for three whole years. But it wasn't what I wanted!

God, did I really just write that? Yeah, I did. Because it's the truth! It wasn't what I wanted! It wasn't even my idea! That first night I didn't do *anything;* we were on the couch and he kind of worked his way behind me gradually; we were sitting there listening to Gregorian Chants, so that seemed really nice, and he was just getting comfortable, right? But then, he was moving his arm around me, more and then a bit more, and then he had his hand on my belt, and I started holding my breath, watching that hand, how it moved under and snaked its way down into me.

God, nothing like those first touches with Andrea! To me she was beautiful fire, but this — this was holding my breath, not feeling anything but a certain shameful horror. He just kept going.

Yaghhhhhhhhh!!!!!!! Those hands! Agghhh! Get away from me!!!! Get away!

OK, OK, take a breath and keep going.

Because I remember a time before that actually, when he tried to get a hold of me that way — we were walking out of the empty Romance Languages office. I was ahead of him and from behind he took my arm by the elbow and I tore it away from him in a lurch and kept walking out the door. We just went down the hall after that. He didn't say anything about it, so neither did I.

But look!!! That first time, in the office, I jerked away! But what the fuck are you supposed to do, when you're all alone at his house and he's got you on the couch and he's just fed you hot chocolate and listened to all your third form worries and he is playing you beautiful monks' music and his home is like a harbor in the world? That's how he got me! Because he was nice to me when no one else was. And he was very smart. And not only that, he was charming; always telling me all those wonderful stories about marching in the sixties and how he used to go traveling across the world, going to places like Tibet and China. I wanted to hang out with him because he was different, not preppy — a James Dean in his own right, someone who took pride in the way he wouldn't conform and he didn't expect me to either. He made me feel OK about being different, made it OK that I didn't fit in at this fucking school. Everybody else was the enemy. My god, that was our battle cry all along. It made me feel so grown up.

But the thing is there have always been a few other kids here who feel the same way, like they don't fit in. I should have been hanging out with them! He could have helped me figure out how to do that. But no, he doesn't fit in either, so he wasn't going to do that. He needed company out on the fringes. Well, damn, I may end up living my life out on the fringes, but I think I could have done without living on his. But back then when I was 14, he was the only thing that looked like what I so desperately needed. That's how he got what he wanted out of me. And *sex* is what he wanted. Fucking.

But it's not what I wanted!!!!! It's not, not, not! It never was.

That *fucker*.

June 3d, 1980 *Wednesday*   5 MORE DAYS

So, so so!!!! I lost my head this morning. In a good way tho. 'Cause it was like I finally saw the thing so clearly — it's just the goddamn Truth! It couldn't be more fucking obvious, anybody can see it!

But how come Bellows can't? How come? I don't get it. I mean what Rik does is wrong. Period. No two ways around it. Maybe I just didn't explain it right. Maybe if I had figured out some other way to approach him —

But no, I've had my shot. It's Mic's turn now. Let a teacher try.

Jesus. What a horrible time I had in that office this morning. I went in so pumped tho, so pumped and so clear. I woke *up* that way, knowing what I had to do. Because I could see it that clearly. And as soon as it was eight, I was on my way to that office, scared to death, but such clarity too! Pounding in me.

Bellows, on the other hand, was so composed when I got in that place. He looked up from where he was sitting, pushed back at his desk, his long legs stretched out in front of him, crossed at the

166

ankles. He gestured to the chair and I sat down, his massive wooden desk a bulwark between us. How come if that guy is already so big, he's got to have a huge desk too? God, you walk into that place and if you're not six feet two, you instantly feel dwarfed. It's weird.

He sat there, arms folded across his wide chest, fresh white shirt, dark blue tie with the Bristol insignia on it; god, they're all perfectly obsessed with this place, you'd think the institution was their mother.

At first, for this one horrible moment, I couldn't say a word. But I looked around me, and saw that I had come this far. No turning back, you know? So I opened my mouth and jumped. Got right to the point — I told him that Andrea was being unfairly punished because what she wrote was true.

CAN YOU BELIEVE I SAID THAT!!!!!!!!!
CHRIST!

Bellows pulled up to his desk to face me. Very big man. He cleared his throat and asked what I could possibly mean by that. I repeated myself exactly, same words. I think this is where I went wrong. I think I should have squeezed in more stuff right then, like the *whole* story summarized really fast so he would have had to see it was the truth. And I *was* opening my mouth then to tell him more, but he was already talking. He told me that once again I wasn't understanding a teacher's position. Speaking as if from some great height. "Now Stephanie, it is difficult to be a young male teacher here, surrounded by multitudes of extremely attractive young girls who love nothing better than your attentions. It's only normal for a man to respond sometimes."

!

That's when I lost my shit. I don't know if I can even describe it, but it was like I couldn't see anything. Like the rug, floor, building, and entire foundation were suddenly gone, yanked away. Nothing to hold on to. Nothing. NOTHING. I blurted out like a drowning person, no consideration for the tactful approach. It's just not what you're thinking about when the waters are closing in over your head. "He seduced me!" I croaked, cried, whispered, screamed, I don't know what. God why didn't I keep my cool!

Bellows leaned all of his massive self towards me over the desk, the full weight of everything behind him — the whole school! — and all of his righteousness in his face. Bearing down on me. I thought he was going to swallow me whole or burn me alive. He started talking in this heavy serious voice, oh but with an edge! — telling me I could not begin to appreciate the gravity of what I was saying, how such reckless accusations were out of place, and that unless I wanted to join my friend on the paint crew and also endanger my already tenuous position at the Bristol School, I had best pocket my words and go on my way. That was all and good morning.

I stared at him. I felt just like the time I was way small and this older person — who was it? I can't even remember, but somebody a whole lot older than me, somebody HUGE — didn't like what I was saying. And where I had been standing on the ground, talking, all of a sudden I was hoisted up into the swimming air by the front of my shirt. YIKES! Whatever it was I had been saying, I took it back.

Bellows didn't say a word more, but pulled his chair forward and bent over the papers spread wide on his desk, his air dismissing me entirely.

I managed to find my legs, which, thank god, still worked, even tho they felt like wooden appendages. Walked stiffly out, stiffly back here to lie on my bed for the longest time, like in shock. Why did I lose all my words like that? What in the world is fucking wrong with me? This paralysis! I lay there and lay there, and I thought maybe I would spin off the planet. I thought maybe even if I didn't, I wished I would. I thought about all the things I should have said to Bellows, all the ways I could have tried to explain it to him, ways maybe even he would have to understand.

God! This school really wouldn't let that kind of shit go on, would it? I mean, if Bellows could really understand what it was like for me, what it did to me? If I could just get him to see THAT! But he thinks I'm just a kid. That's what I started to get. How he can't hear that stuff from a kid. It has to be from someone he respects. It has to be from another teacher.

That's when I ran over to Mic's. Jesus. And now she's going to try. It still makes me crazy that I couldn't do it myself, but I guess I can ask for help. And I know Mic is good help too. I know she'll get him to see if anyone can.

But god, it's not like it was a snap breaking into it with her. She was so tired when I got there. I could see it in her face. I've never known her so tired, almost like caved in. I felt instantly bad, like I shouldn't be throwing more garbage on top of her. But there's nobody else who can help me now! So yeah, I told her. She sat on the couch, and I sat on the floor. I was swimming with the stuff, and I just let it all flow out. I could see Mic starting to come back to herself as I talked, that old fighting spirit filling her again. I told her first about the prank, and then I worked my way backwards. All the way to the beginning. That first night with Rik three and a half years ago. She listened. I felt a little like I had just ripped my shirt off, and she was going to be grossed out for sure. I've been so worried since this shit hit the fan that she thought I was a slut.

She just listened, didn't take her eyes from my face once. Finally she said she'd somehow known all along.

And then — ! what else she said! She said it wasn't my fault!

It's not my fault! It's NOT my fault!

See, she really gets it! She gets it better than me even!

I told her what had happened with Bellows. "Jesus," she said. I asked her, I practically begged her, to go talk with him herself. I told her it wasn't just me, now it's Jeanie too. She wanted to know if I knew that for a fact and I told her that neither of them had actually told me, but that I could see it anyway. She said that probably wouldn't be proof enough for Bellows, but she imagined it would concern him.

Then she said she had to get back to grading.

But that she would go first thing tomorrow morning to talk to Bellows. I thanked her and came back here.

Hoorah for Mic! I knew she wouldn't let me down!

— But damn I just remembered that she didn't say a word about my story! Maybe she didn't like it? Maybe it was too much. Or maybe the ending gives her the creeps, two girls going off together like that. God maybe I should have left that part out.

Who knows. But don't worry about it now. Think about this instead, the way she said those three years weren't my fault at all. That they were Rik's fault. That he's the teacher and the responsibility is on him to maintain "appropriate relationships" with students.

Wow.

June 4th, 1980 *Thursday* 4 MORE DAYS

So she says she can't do anything! Nothing! I went up there to talk to her, and she was all caved in again. Mic, Mic, Mic! Talk to me! I could see it on her face, it's no use. She can't deal! She can't, can't, because —

God, I can't stand seeing her this way. She's so tired, even more tired than yesterday morning, old like I don't even know her. Please, please, come back to life Mic and talk to me. Don't let him make it into perverted stuff Mic. Mic! Don't die on me! I'm counting on you! You're the one who said wear your insides out, and now where the hell are you? God, she's gone. Drowned.

I'm crying now as I write this. Me. Crying. Here I sit, piles of packing all around me, these ruins of my life from the last four years, and I have to keep stopping just to breathe and wipe the water off my cheeks. It's all over, all over. And what did any of it amount to? Not one piece lasted, it all turned sour, every last bit. Granite and Rik and Andrea and now even Mic.

How could she? Was I just imagining that last part today? I don't know, by the end of my time up in her apartment, I could have been hallucinating, I don't know.

She told me she was sorry but there was nothing she could do. But that was a lie. I knew she wasn't sorry, she was just past all feeling, she was like some walking dead person. I could see it! But I asked her what had happened anyway. And she told me. Told me that Bellows had just dismissed my "accusations." And when she had tried pressing him, explaining how I had come to her, had already shared confidences, how she thought she had grounds for believing me, he had bristled, told her he had known me quite a bit longer and was therefore in a better position to judge my character.

Mic would hardly look at me as she told me this stuff. She was standing by her window, looking out towards Rt. 8. Her place was the messiest I have ever seen it, papers and clothes strewn around everywhere, coffee mugs and plates on the floor. An open letter on the table and next to it that framed photo that last time was by her bed. Well.

After that bit about my "character," Mic stopped talking. I waited, wanting to cry, to scream. Waited and waited. Finally just said her name, and she turned towards me, this strange flash of pain going across her face. I think I knew then that we were in bigger trouble than I had even guessed before. But I didn't know what it was!

So I said, "Mic, you didn't even stick up for me!"

She said Bellows had made it impossible. I asked her what that meant, and god! that's when the trouble showed itself in the room. Her words. "He insinuated certain things about your relationship with Andrea, Stevie." I felt the hot flush across my face; my arms and legs all surging with this feeling of being CAUGHT. I didn't say anything. I couldn't have. Struck dumb.

Mic was looking back out the window. I think she wanted to be out on that road, heading away, far away. Me, I stood there in her kitchen, grinding my foot into the floor, feeling like my cover had just been ripped off.

But standing there, feeling like the dirtiest thing in the world, I suddenly remembered how it was Mic who had given me Rubyfruit when I had asked for it, how her friend had even written about that stuff in her paper! I burst out, full of all that. "What about Rubyfruit, Mic? What about your friend Susan? Wasn't it her point that it was OK to be different? What about that Mic? I thought you believed in that kind of stuff!"

She shot me a look, almost like I had slapped her. I took a step back. Yeah, I wanted her to feel what I was saying, but I didn't want it to hit her like that either. I looked at her, and for the first time I saw the red in her eyes. Like she'd been crying maybe? She looked away from me, out the window. Then she turned fast and walked to the table. Sat down. Started folding up the letter. Closing things up, that's what was happening on her face. Something in me screamed.

"Mic! Wear your insides out!"

God, I said it out loud.

She answered me in a tight voice, looking down at the table. She told me that I had no idea what it was like for her in Bellows' office, that she would have lost all credibility as a teacher if she had spoken out against his comment. "He would have laughed in my face, Stevie. You don't know!" She pointed to the photo. "You're just like Susan, you know that!"

Susan! It's Susan in the photo with her! Inside I jumped, something lurched to a startled attention.

But she, meanwhile, was going on, about how she couldn't very well say the kinds of things at Bristol that Susan could write in her thesis. "He would have sneered me out of his office Stevie! You don't know what it's like. This is an extremely conservative school! I mean, the next thing you know, he would be making insinuations about me!"

And the thing in me that had jumped to its feet stomped inside me, and I looked at her and I, me, Stevie the meek, kind of lost it. I sort of started raving, going on and on about how that would be just talk, and talk couldn't hurt her; sticks and stones can break your bones but words can never hurt you kind of thing. On and on. I was way out beyond myself.

So yeah, I guess I pissed her off! Maybe I got

what I deserved then. By this time she had stuffed the letter into the envelope it had come in. I could see her name scrawled across the front and "The Bristol School" done in over-fancy letters.

"You really don't understand, do you Stevie? It's not the truth that matters around this place! Just talk could do me in!"

"But no Mic! It's still just talk! Shit, I know everybody has been talking about me all along! And about Rik too! Jesus! He's a teacher! And all that talk doesn't touch him! And Christ, with him, it was true! Think what a better position you'd be in!"

Mic stood up, fast and tight. "Look Stevie, it's not a position I'm going to put myself in! Get that thru your head."

I finally saw that she meant it. I stood there, just looking at her. She wouldn't look back. I thought I was going to cry any second, something in me bursting to the surface, need tearing out of me. "Why not Mic?! Why not?!"

That's when she asked me to leave. !!!! She said she was sorry, but still, she kicked me out, that's the truth. And she just wouldn't look me in the face either. She was holding the letter tucked inside her sweatshirt pocket and with her other hand she picked up the picture. Started down the hall. Saying something about how she needed to be alone. How she was sorry, but we were just spinning in circles, neither of us being able to understand the other; we obviously weren't going to get anywhere.

So I left.

I wasn't going to cry either. And I didn't. 'Cause you know what, she's wrong! I think I do understand her!!! Maybe I'm crazy, but I think I do!

I mean, it was her friend Susan in that photo. Not a sister at all! And she keeps the thing by her bed! And I bet you that was a letter from Susan too! I bet it was! And that's not all I bet! But how could she just sit there with Bellows like that if it's true! How could she! But I think it is true.

I think mic is JUST LIKE ME!

mic!

June 5th, 1980 *Friday*   3 MORE DAYS

God. I woke up crying this morning. Crying! And the funny thing is, it felt good! Like the way sneezing or getting a big gulp of air feels good. So I just kept crying, me and the wet on my face. Then I wanted to GET UP! I swung out of bed, feet on the floor, and the tears were still coming, but I was sort of laughing too, I don't know, I was coming awake, this strange mix of sorrow and joy aching in me. I pulled on my jeans and red T-shirt and that beat up cranberry-colored sweatshirt and out the door, I didn't even know where to. But walking down the hall, I noticed I felt hungry and so I headed for the dining hall. On the way over I bought a Coke from the vending machines, and once I got to the dining hall I saw it was nearly ten! A lot later than I thought! I slipped thru the empty hall over to the side bar and slapped some P&J on some of that marshmallow stuff that's a lame excuse for bread. Ambled out the other door, into the coffee room. And surprise, surprise, there at the corner back table, *our* corner back table, were Liddy and Duncan. Playing a game of chess.

Duncan said, "Hey Roughgarden! Long time, no see! C'mon over here, I miss your face." I walked towards them, feeling like I'd just arrived from somewhere very far away, another planet maybe. Still — I was willing to land. So, I sat backwards on one of the red chairs, my chest leaning into its hardwood back.

"Playing some chess, huh?" I said. How about that for suave.

"Yeah, and I'm winning," said Liddy.

"I'm just stringing you along, don't you worry," said Duncan moving this one piece — I forget what it is — to the left so that it lined up with Liddy's queen, "Check, chicky."

"What?" I said, "How do you get that?"

"Oh, that's right, you haven't seen the way we play," said Liddy, scooting her queen to the right.

"What way?"

"We reverse the queen and king, so it's the queen you got to checkmate," said Liddy. Duncan had propped her head in her hands and was studying the board.

"Oh!"

"Do you like that?" asked Duncan, swiveling her head in her hands towards me.

Well, I couldn't help grinning, it just got me. Here these two girls could sit in this room and play a thing just the way they wanted, turning it around to suit them. I did like it. I told them I liked it.

That's when we got talking of course. It always happens you know. And this time I didn't even mind that we got into hairy stuff. Tho I did get sort of nervy at first. But still — it's what I needed to do to make the break back to you-know-who. (Yes, yes, yes!)

It was Duncan who brought it up this time. That sort of surprised me. Liddy's the one who's been doing the nudging. It's just more like her. But this time, no, it was Duncan. She was still looking at the board, but she asked me, "So look Stevie, tell me if it isn't any of my business, but what's the story anyway with your bud? Did she really write that stuff and glue all the doors too? All by herself?"

I made a sweep of the place. It was empty. I knew that, but I was just making sure. What the hell, we're out of here Sunday, I thought. Then I told them no, told Duncan and Liddy the story of the four of us, Andrea and Eliot and Ken, setting out, and how Andry, after a while, had taken off.

"I can't say that surprises me," said Liddy dryly, "God, she took the whole rap tho."

Duncan was looking at me, a question forming on her face. Not just any question. THE question. Then she saw me looking at her, and she looked away. We made this small talk for a few minutes about what a drag it must be for Andrea to be painting when the rest of us are hanging out. I could see that they were both wondering, but they weren't going to push me! If I wanted, I could hold my tongue and leave it at that. I sat there with them, feeling my silence, feeling how deep and wide it really is, how it is just another thing you can drown in. I really got it — the drowning you do when you can't tell the truth. I felt my breath catching in my throat. So I opened my mouth to breathe and next thing I knew I was speaking it,

"What she wrote on those walls is true, you know." I sat, looking at Liddy's dark queen, not at either of them.

"I knew it!" exclaimed Liddy.

"That slimeball!" said Duncan.

And because Duncan is right — Rik is a slimeball — I plunged into the whole story, everything that I should have told Bellows the other day but couldn't, 'cause, hell he wasn't even listening! He didn't want to hear it! That's the thing! You know, just telling the story to someone who is really listening, who wants to hear and understands it, helps you see when someone isn't, doesn't, won't.

So I told them everything, from how it started way back in third form year, how needy I was back then, to how he took advantage of that all along.

"That's how he works, you know," said Duncan.

"How he works?" I echoed her.

"Remember, my dad's been working here for twenty years, Stevie. Hell, he warned me to steer clear of Rik!"

"He did?"

"Yup," Duncan went on, "My dad thinks Rik should leave the girls alone."

"You mean you already knew — ?"

"Don't let it get to you, Stevie," said Liddy. "You're right, he really slimed you into it."

"Look on the bright side," said Duncan, "It turned out OK anyway, right? I mean, Andrea's your friend now, right?"

I was sitting there, letting it all wash over me.

OK, OK, so some people saw that, but it didn't kill me. I know I'm not dirty, and that's the most important thing. And now I am out of it — free! *And* Andrea *is* my friend. Well, I was hoping she might be. I started nodding, nodding hard.

"She's my friend all right," I said, "my very good friend. I love her."

"Well there you go," said Duncan. Liddy was nodding too. I smiled sort of funny at them, kind of embarrassed, but kind of happy too. They knew! And it was OK. Jesus, why can't the whole school be like them? Why can't the whole world?

So I sat there a while longer with them, finishing my Coke and watching them play chess. Then I knew what I had to do. I got up, gave them my thanks, and took off for the Sports Center.

I had a hard time finding her at first. I looked and looked, but she wasn't there, she wasn't there. The swimming pool wasn't where I expected she'd be, but finally I checked there anyway, dashing up the steps and swinging the door wide — to see her. For a moment I simply stood, looking in my surprise: the pool entirely drained, so empty, like a huge gaping mouth and Andry way at the bottom in the deep end with a paint roller on a pole. But the strangest thing was this mask she was wearing, this thing that covered her whole face. Looked sort of like a gas mask. For a second I thought maybe it wasn't her after all. It could have been anyone — a space alien or a soldier under there. But then she pulled the thing up, and I saw her, red marks around her nose and mouth.

I walked in and stopped again. We stood there, looking at each other, me standing at the edge, her on the other end from me, roller in hand.

"Hi," I said finally. Christ, was I nervous! What if she blew me off! Told me to go fuck myself. "How's it going?"

Andrea, my friend, my very good friend whom I love! shrugged. "I figure it's good practice for the summer," she said.

"Huh. So you got the paint crew together then?" I asked. Filling up the space.

"More or less." She was looking at me. I saw then that she was waiting. Waiting to see why I had come, waiting to see what I had in me, I think.

I couldn't say it yet. Instead I asked if there was another roller, another mask.

"You want to help?" she asked. "Why?"

"Because," I said. "Because. Will you let me?"

She shrugged again, put the roller down and went off for a few minutes. Came back with a roller, a mask, a little brush, and a small can of dark blue paint. When I asked her what that was for, she told me it was touch up paint for the walls.

So I strapped that mask on and went down with her. We started working. Just working, not even talking for I don't know, maybe twenty minutes. That felt a little funny, like what was she thinking of me. But then too it felt so good to be next to her again anyway, to feel the rhythm of her body as she worked alongside me. God how I love her! But seeing too that steeliness in her as she worked, that piece in her that just goes at things. The piece that really annoys me in her sometimes! So I was feeling that too. Feeling her. All of her, even the parts I could probably never find the words for.

Finally I just said thru the mask, "Andrea!"

She didn't even stop. "What?"

"I've missed you," I said. I didn't know how else to put it.

Now she stopped. Looked at me. It was weird, the two of us standing at the bottom of that pool, looking out at each other thru these floppy masks.

"Funny way to show it!" she said thru her mask.

She was mad! I thought that would be it then. I stood up in mid-stroke. But then she was going on.

"I mean, I know you were really upset and everything, but you didn't have to go and make like I didn't even exist Stevie! Don't you know how that made me feel!" She wasn't looking at me, still painting, her movements jerky. But how the hell was I supposed to have known how she was feeling? It made me mad back.

"What about the way I was feeling Andrea? How would you like it if the whole school knew some teacher was screwing you!"

"That wasn't the point, Stevie!"

"Yeah right!"

She whipped her mask off then, stood facing me, her face bared, sweaty, her curls sticking to her forehead. We stood there, her eyes locking me in.

"What do you want from me!" I cried out.

"I want you to take that damn mask off! I want to see you!"

I didn't want to take that damn mask off at all! I paused, turned my head. "Stevie!" Anger and pleading turning in her voice. I pulled the thing off.

But I couldn't look at her. I knew she wanted me to even tho she didn't say so. I could feel it in her, could feel her in me. Finally I looked. She was looking right at me. I turned away, then looked again.

"Stevie, I love you dammit! I wrote that shit on the wall because I love you!"

"That's a pretty strange way to show it!" I said. "Tell the whole school I'm a slut!"

"I don't think you're a slut, Stevie!"

Oh god. Oh god. "Yes you do!"

"I think Rik is a lecher. That's what I wrote, isn't it!?"

"What's that make me then?"

"His prey, dammit Stevie!"

I was looking away again by this time of course. But yeah, I was getting it. It's the same thing I've come to see myself. Just I got so nervous that she wasn't going to think of it that way. But this is Andrea! Andrea who understands me like nobody else. Andrea.

Still without looking, but all the fight gone out of my voice, I started telling her about that night at the Senior Dance. Started in slow, all the while studying my sneakers, scuffed old things. They sure should be more interesting than they are for all the time I spend looking at them! I talked and talked. I told her everything I saw. I told her about that first nite, how he snaked into me. And then I was looking at her, and I could see how she was listening, taking my story in, really hearing it.

"Stevie," she said, and then I was in her arms. Finally! The place I love best in the world. She held me and held me. And I think I cried a little.

God, I want to leave it at that. But there's one more piece I got to put down in here! How after a bit of that, we finished up the painting and went to the snack bar. And how when we came back the paint was all dry, and from where I stood, that pool suddenly looked like a huge blank page. This idea jumped into my mind and I went and grabbed that little can of paint.

"Time for an art project," I said, prying up the lid and stirring it with the paint stick, watching the lighter and darker colors melding into one river of blue. Picked up the little brush next to the can and swung down the ladder. Knelt down in the deep end.

Andrea was walking up behind me, asking, "What are you doing?" I kept painting, and she mouthed the letters from over my shoulder. "R," she said, "I. K. W. O. O. D. I. S. A. L. E. C! H! E! R!" And we were laughing together, laughing in that way when it comes right up out your very gut. I kept on writing, repeating that line and the other one that Andrea wrote before too: "Rik Wood preys on students." Then Andrea took a turn. We decorated the whole bottom of that deep end. First thing tomorrow morning they're filling it, and Andrea says she's sure they won't be checking the paint job. So that writing is going to be there for some time to come! It's there. A message for all Bristol swimmers! The truth down under.

*June 6th, 1980 *Saturday* THE DAY BEFORE!

Rik —

I bet you didn't expect to get a letter from me. I bet you didn't think you would hear from me at all.

But you are.

I want you to know that I know what you are doing with Jeanie, that I know who you are. That no matter how many nice words you cover it with, you *are* a lecher. That you *do* prey on students.

It took me a long time to see this. I wanted to believe you when you called it love. But I know now that it wasn't love. Love would have been keeping your hands off me, love would have been listening to me and giving me advice — like the way Mic does! — and leaving it at that. Love would have been letting me grow up in my own time, not your time, not getting sex out of me. I never told you how I felt about that first time, did I? I didn't like it! But I thought it was my fault for not working right. And that's what I thought for a long time. But now I know that I do work, that it can feel right to me.

That leer you gave me and Andrea on the dance floor was disgusting. And that crack you made to Andrea about her sculpture! You are a disgusting man! You call something disgusting love and then try to make love look like something disgusting.

All you think about is what you want. You never even asked me if I liked that stuff you did. I never thought to ask myself. I thought I had to make you happy. But I didn't like it! What I liked was your

185

attention. I wanted you to care about me, ME, not my sex. Damn you for that first night you trapped me on the couch. Why didn't you get your slimy hands off me! Damn you for every time I had to go thru that shit with you in bed. And specially damn you for that last time, the way you were so slow to roll off me, even tho I was *begging* you to get off. Who the hell do you think you are! I asked you to get off me. Why did I have to beg! You should have listened to me right away!

And now you are doing the same shit to Jeanie. You are really gross. Andrea was right to write those things on your wall. She knows all about you, you know. So does Mic. She agrees with me too. And I even went in to Bellows to try and tell him about it. But you're safe, you know that. You know he won't listen to me. You know that he is protecting your ass because around this fucked-up place, your ass is more important than mine, even when you're doing something wrong. I don't know why this is the case, but I sure found that it is. You know that, and I know you think you're safe, no matter how many of us you seduce. But you just wait — someday you're going to find out you're wrong. Dead wrong. Even if Bellows protects your ass your whole life long, someday you're going to wake up and find your soul has rotted because of all the lies you've lived.

And I won't feel a bit sorry for you.

In truth,

Stevie

June 7th, 1980 *Sunday*   I AM GRADUATED

Well, this is about it for this book — I'm almost out of pages and I think it's about time for a new one anyway. This last day has to be told tho, I think.

So — here I am at Andrea's, and we're going to take it easy this week, maybe go to a few graduation parties, maybe not, before we start on the paint crew. Lois is cool about me being here for now. We'll go up to Vermont next weekend, get my stuff and come back down. I might move in for the summer with some of these other girls that Andrea knows — they're getting this whole big house. Could be really fun! Tho in a way I want to stay right here with her. Still. I kind of would like my own room too. But we'll see. I don't have to decide anything tonight!

Well. It happened. Graduation. We sat there in the big gym and we heard all the speeches. I didn't like it. And that's putting it mildly! I sat there in that stiff white dress Mom and Oma got me, and I listened to Bellows saying that Bristol's priority is its students. My ass!!! Yeah, exactly. My ass. Yuk. Can you believe that shit. I'm so glad I am out of that place. Tho I don't quite believe it yet!

And then there were all the parents. They came in droves, in station wagons with fake wooden sides and in big dark cars. Pressed and perfumed masses, elegant rich adults, full of anxious pride.

God, I am sooo glad I am out of that place!

Then my parents of course. Oma and Opa to cut the tension between them. Oh god, my parents. I think I'll save really writing about them for the next journal!

So, what else? Oh yeah, Mic! I was walking towards Warnock to meet Lois and Andrea so we could leave, and she came out the front door of Academy. I was going to pretend I hadn't seen her! But she called my name. Came towards me. And when she was a couple of feet away, she stopped. At first she didn't say anything, just stood there, looking at me. What was in her face! Some sadness, something proud, something tender, but something else not letting go?

I don't know what was in my face, but looking right at her like that, I saw how beautiful she is. Oh Mic! What about going the way your blood beats? But I didn't say that. Finally she said she wished me luck. I said I wished her the same.

And that was just about it. I had to go. I told her Andrea was waiting for me. She said goodbye. I said goodbye. But then as I was turning to go, she said, "Stevie!" I turned to look back at her, and she said she wished the two of us the best.

"Thanks Mic," I said. Then I left. But I felt so sad walking the path back down to Warnock! I don't know. There's so much! But no matter what, she did teach me a lot. And I am going to miss her. And always remember her.

I don't want to write anymore about it tho. About her. What I want to write about is my real graduation! The little ceremony Andrea and I gave each other last night. I suppose if I'm going to tell the story right tho, I should start with that little Hop we had last night in the Snack Bar. Williams was the one who got the key and got us all in there. He is pretty cool. He's the teacher that likes to have fun. And there were about twenty of us in there. Those of us not still out having dinner with our parents or partying in the woods. I was happy. Andrea was there with me, and Liddy and Duncan were there and Sylvie and Val and Ken and Eliot and Diamond too. Plus a bunch more. Some of the people I've liked best here. Some of the ones I wished I'd gotten to know better.

But anyway, we were dancing and dancing, and it was so fun. Me and Andrea even danced a slow one and nobody seemed even to blink. And about half way thru, out waltzed Liddy and Duncan, arm in arm! Well, well, you just never know, do you? But you can guess all right!

My guess is yes. Andrea's too.

But anyway, while she and I were dancing, we decided we would spend our last night at Bristol in bed together. Whispering the plan back and forth as we swayed to "Peaceful Easy Feeling." Oh! I felt the warmth growing in me for her!

And that's what we did. Oh god. She came to my room. And it was the first time we've been together since the whole mess came down, so it was kind of like not eating for a while, how you get hungry. I lit about five candles and turned off the lights. And we went.

I know I have never gone so far in my life. Not so much what we did, but someplace I went farther than ever before in myself, reaching for her, feeling her reaching for me.

How do I put this? It's the most important thing in this whole book! How I feel. How much I feel! Jesus, I am not broke!

Her. Feeling her touch in me, the way she moved all up and down the length of me. I felt her all the way thru, down into a place I didn't even know was there. Must be the place where love lives. Yeah. That's it. The place where love lives. And then, sleep came so easy, drifting down into it, dreaming the whole night long. Dreaming that old dream of Kit! I can see her up in that big old pine, and I'm walking towards her, the whole time calling out her name. This time I finally get to the tree. Kit is climbing down, meowing and then she's in my arms and we're walking and walking, walking right up until I woke up and there was Andrea next to me, sleeping, burrowed in. I looked at her, coming to, feeling how that cat had just been cuddled in against my chest, purring.

"Andrea!"

I whispered her name. And without really coming awake exactly, she moved across the bed into my arms. And we lay there like that, for the longest time, not really awake, not worrying yet about the day ahead of us, the time behind us, not worrying about any of it. Just lying there. In our own time. Hers and mine.